Sidney Perley

The Poets of Essex County

Massachusetts

Sidney Perley

The Poets of Essex County
Massachusetts

ISBN/EAN: 9783743463547

Manufactured in Europe, USA, Canada, Australia, Japa

Cover: Foto ©Andreas Hilbeck / pixelio.de

Manufactured and distributed by brebook publishing software (www.brebook.com)

Sidney Perley

The Poets of Essex County

THE

POETS

OF

ESSEX COUNTY.

MASSACHUSETTS.

By SIDNEY PERLEY,

Author of "History of Boxford, Mass.;" "Goodridge Memorial;" etc.

Poetry! the gem that gilds
The world of letters, and gives
Expression to soul beauty.

SALEM, MASS.:
SIDNEY PERLEY.
1889.

PRINTED AT THE SALEM PRESS.

PREFACE.

"**O**F the dignity of Poetry," says Camden, in his *Remains*, "much hath bene faid by the worthy Sir *Philip Sidney*, & by the Gentleman which proued that Poets were the firſt *Politicians*, the firſt *Philoſophers*, the firſt *Hiſtoriographers*. I will onely adde out of *Philo*, that they were Gods owne creatures, who in his Booke *de Plantatione Noe*, reporteth, that when he had made the whole worlds maſſe ; he created Poets to celebrate & ſet out the Creator himſelfe, and all the Creatures : you Poets read the place and you will like it."

Although we may not fully agree with the ancient writers, it is indeed true that poets occupy no insignificant position. If we believe the words of Fletcher of Saltoun, when he says, " Let who will make the laws of a nation if I may write its songs, " there must be some power in poetry stronger than the judiciary itself in the control of that nation. The poet Whittier made

" . . . . his rustic reed of song
A weapon in the war with wrong."

(3)

And the poet Massey strings his lyre

> " For the cause that lacks assistance,
> For the wrong that needs resistance,
> For the future in the distance,
> And the good that he can do. "

They deserve an equal honor with our statesmen and historians, and our clergymen, too, if we believe, with Longfellow, that

> " God sent his singers upon earth
> With songs of sadness and of mirth,
> That they might touch the hearts of men,
> And bring them back to heaven again. "

Much has been published in Essex county relating to its prose writers, and its statesmen and theologians, but very little concerning its poets. This seemed a gap in our literature that ought to be filled, and it has been our endeavor to supply that want by this little volume of short biographical sketches of our verse writers and selections from their productions.

Most of our spare time during the last nine years has been given to this work ; and an almost incredible amount of labor has been performed in the reading and criticism of probably ten thousand poems, and in extensive correspondence and research for the discovery of writers and for biographical material before the preparation of the volume could be begun.

SIDNEY PERLEY.

Salem, Mass., Dec. 31, 1888.

THE POETS OF ESSEX COUNTY.

A new country produces very little ornamental literature,—the rough life of frontiersmen tending from such pursuits. New England was no exception to this rule. Engaged in clearing the forest and tilling the barren soil with their few and rude implements, securing for themselves food, clothing and shelter, and ever on the alert lest the Indians should surprise and massacre the household, the time and abilities of the early settlers were consumed. Isolated from each other they lacked the mental growth and strength and culture that mind in contact with mind obtains; and with little or no means of education, the growth of a literary life was necessarily very slow. And yet from its earliest settlement, Essex county had its literary people who published more or less. Anne Bradstreet wrote here early in the seventeenth century, as also did the famous Nathaniel Ward, author of "The Simple Cobbler of Agawam." As the country grew older war after war disturbed its life, reducing its strength and culture, and hindering that natural literary growth which was the legitimate result of our later school system. The orna-

mental had appeared in our literature to a limited extent only. After the close of the Revolution, education
began a new era. Schools and colleges multiplied in
number and improved in quality. At this juncture poetry in our literature becomes prominent. Since that
time the number of writers has constantly and greatly
increased ; and in Essex county alone there have been
several hundred writers of poetry, most of whom have
published their efforts in contemporary periodical literature. The names of many early versifiers are lost on
account of their poems having been published anonymously, or under assumed names ; and still earlier we
cannot doubt there were many writers of poetry of whom
we have never learned,—who wrote but never published
their productions. The local newspapers have been to
a great extent the occasion of the large number of modern writers. Their columns are open to any local effort
that is of passable quality ; and the interest and ambition thus engendered and fostered have caused new and
special endeavors to be taken in this direction. In such
ways began to write Whittier, Emerson, and other poets
of our day.

Among the numerous prose writers of Essex county
it was but natural that there should be those who could
write in measure and with rhythm. From Nathaniel
Hawthorne, the greatest American novelist, down
through the line of lesser writers of fiction ; from Hubbard and Prescott, the historians, and other contribu-
tors to our historical literature ; from Ward and Story,
the authors of treatises on the law ; and from other

writers of many books on art, science and theology, poets have come to complete the canon of our literature.

Nearly all of the great American poets have some
connection with Essex county. At Newbury, in an old
mansion lately standing, the great-grandfather of Longfellow was born ; and at the Jonathan Johnson house at
Nahant his "Song of Hiawatha" was written. James
Russell Lowell also traces his family back to old Newbury, where his lineal ancestors lived for several generations ; and Ralph Waldo Emerson is a direct descend-
ant of the Ipswich family of that name.

There were several distinguished writers, who resided
here for so short a time as hardly to have become resi-
dents, and are therefore not properly admissible to this
volume. Among them was President John Q. Adams,
who studied law in Newburyport, and while there wrote
some good hymns. He afterwards contributed poetry
to *The Token*, and other publications. The celebrated
Robert Treat Paine, son of the signer of the Declaration
of Independence of that name, also studied law in Newburyport, in the office of Theophilus Parsons. He
made his name immortal by writing, in 1798, at the age
of twenty-five, his celebrated national song, entitled
"Adams and Liberty," beginning,

" Ye sons of Columbia who so bravely have fought
   For those rights which unstained from your sires had descended,
May you long taste the blessings your valor has bought,
   And your sons reap the soil which your fathers defended !
            'Mid the reign of mild peace
            May your nation increase

With the glory of Rome and the wisdom of Greece !
And ne'er shall the sons of Columbia be slaves
While the earth bears a plant, or the sea rolls its waves."

Nathaniel Parker Willis was an early summer resident at Nahant, and Oliver Wendell Holmes at Beverly Farms. At Manchester have resided James T. Fields, Richard H. Dana, and James Freeman Clarke.

The poets of Essex county have published a number of pamphlets and one hundred and forty bound volumes of poems. They have clothed their thoughts in many forms, and produced many varieties of poetry,—hymns, lyrics, idyls, songs, epics, satires, dramas, and occasional poems. With some the sonnet has been the favorite form, and a few have written in blank verse.

The county has been particularly favored by its many sweet singers, whose words cheer the heart stricken with sorrow, give variety and a fulness and finish to the literary exercises of public gatherings, prevent their spread by showing in a pleasing way the error or shallowness of certain popular customs and opinions, give a greater and more varied effect to our stage, and in hymns reach the heart of the outcast, cheer the world-weary soul, and furnish a medium of praise to the object of our worship. The spirit of freedom is breathed as a part of the life of the people, and it has gone out in songs to cheer and support and stir up the inhabitants of other lands in battling for liberty. Our songs rang through the camps in the Revolution, and inspired the disheartened soldiers in the war of the Rebellion.

The abolition of slavery in our country was largely due to our poets,—Whittier, Garrison, and others.

Our storied valleys and hills and streams have furnished themes for the lyric and idyl. Our hills and rivers and ocean are grand and inspiring, and over them all are the beautiful colors and diversity of form and arrangement of the clouds, which make our sunrises and sunsets in delicacy and deepness of color and grandeur without a rival.

OUR HERITAGE.

Belovéd Essex ! thy prolific soil
  Hath nurtured statesmen, jurists, bards divine !
  Thy earnest workers here reveal a mine
Of intellectual wealth ! the meed of toil
Exalted far above the weary moil
  For bare material gain ! They still the wine
  Of high existence ! the quintessence fine
Of ripest thought, that Time can ne'er despoil !
Here nature, opulent, on every hand
  Spreads rarest loveliness in scenes that bind
The heart in strong attachment to the land !
  Yet Essex doth her highest glory find
In lofty flights of inspiration grand,
  And the immortal triumphs of the mind !

ABEL G. COURTIS.

Lynn, December, 1888.

SKETCHES AND POEMS.

WILLIAM PAGE ANDREWS.

M R. ANDREWS was born in Framingham, Mass., November 22, 1848, and was son of Samuel Page and Rebecca Bacon (Scudder) Andrews. When William was four years of age, the family removed to Salem, where they have since resided. He was educated in the public schools of Salem, and by private instruction. After the completion of his education, he was for some years a clerk in a merchant's counting-room in Boston. When the First District court of Essex county, located at Salem, was established in 1874, his father was made clerk and Mr. Andrews was appointed assistant clerk thereof. This office he continued to hold until the resignation of his father in April, 1888, when he was made clerk and his father assistant clerk. Mr. Andrews has written book notices and other prose articles, and contributed poems to *The Century*, and other magazines, and to the *Salem Gazette, Christian Register, Boston Transcript, New York Critic*, and other papers. He has also edited

"Poems by Charles T. Brooks" and "Poems by Jones Very," contributing to the last named a memoir. He is favorably known as a translator of the poems of Heine, Rückert, and Göethe, and also of Victor Hugo's writings. His translations of German hymns have appeared in the *Christian Register.* His favorite poets are Shelley, Wordsworth, Keats, and Matthew Arnold.

MATTHEW ARNOLD.

Austere, sedate, the chisel in his hand,
    He carved his statue from a flawless stone,
    That faultless verse, whose earnest undertone
Echoes the music of his Grecian land.
Like Sophocles on that Ægean strand
    He walked by night, and watched life's sea alone,
    Amid a temperate, not the tropic zone,
Girt round by cool waves and a crystal sand.
And yet the world's heart in his pulses stirred ;
    He looked abroad across life's wind-swept plain,
And many a wandering mariner has heard
    His warning hail, and as the blasts increase,
Has listened, till he passed the reefs again,
    And floated safely in his port of Peace.

NOVEMBER.

"O bare November !" sings a poet friend,
    Who longs for gladness of a vanished May.
    Look round about you, poet, think, and say :
Did May more shining hours, more beauty, send?

See ! how the softened colors gently blend
  With tenderer harmonies against the gray ;
  How gorgeously the pomp of passing day
Flames through the sky to celebrate its end !
The year is dying ! yes, as old faiths die,
  Chastened and glorified with purer light.
Its flowers have faded ; but the winter, nigh,
  Comes, bringing in their stead a robe of white.
Serene and calm and friendlier, from on high,
  The nearer stars look down more clear and bright.

DARIUS BARRY.

MR. BARRY was born in Haverhill, Mass., December
12, 1812, and was son of John and Susan (Silver) Barry.
In his boyhood he had but few advantages for study,
but his great natural ability has to a large degree supplied the want of education. In 1830, he went to
Charlestown, and remained there two years. He then
went to Lynn, and soon after engaged in the manufacture of morocco, which business he has pursued to the
present time. For one whose life has been so arduous,
he has accomplished a great amount of reading, and
what he has read his strong memory has retained. He
takes a lively interest in current matters, and is an able
debater on all questions of a philosophical or religious
character. His broad and often quaint humor has improved with his age, and has become one of his most
prominent characteristics. His published verses have

been few in number, and have alone appeared originally in the *Lynn Transcript.* He has the true poetic
spirit, and his style is simple and natural, having a delicate descriptive touch, and a due appreciation of the
beautiful.

MORNING.

Upon the world the god of day
   Has burst in rosy light ;
His unseen fingers gather up
   The curtains of the night.

Now up the east, with blazing shield,
   He climbs the dizzy height ;
And hides the fainting stars within
   The mantle of his light.

His warm rays light the hills and streams ;
   The vales his glory share ;
The gray old rocks, on mountain tops,
   His golden garments wear.

The ear drinks in the low sweet sound
   Of murmuring brooks and rills ;
And saffron blushes of the morn
   Fall soft along the hills.

EUGENE BARRY.

MR. BARRY was born in Lynn, Mass., October 12, 1843, and was son of Darius and Jane Hatch (Clark) Barry. Darius Barry, the father, is the subject of the preceding sketch. The son was educated in the Lynn public schools, and graduated from the high school, being the valedictorian of his class. During the period of his school life, he learned the business of morocco manufacturing, and after leaving school continued to work at it. In 1867, he engaged in the business for himself, and has continued in it to the present time. Mr. Barry married, and has addressed to his children some appropriate little poems. Until 1886, he had not printed verses, but since that time has contributed poems to the *Boston Transcript*, and other papers, which have been deservedly popular. He has the laudable ambition to excel, and endeavors to produce something that is akin to the highest type of poetry. He labors over and studies his lines as he prepares them, and has the success of not displaying in them the labored style of composition. He has a talent that will some day express itself yet more clearly.

THE WATER-LILY.

As in the city's dust and heat
  I walked with footsteps sad,
I chanced to see, beside the street,
Close to the throng of hurrying feet,
  A little country lad.

The freedom of the mountain air
   Shone from his sun-lit eye ;
His slender hands held, fresh and fair,
A bunch of water-lilies rare
   To tempt the passer by.

'Twas but a glance, yet strangely sweet,
   Its spell my heart beguiled.
I saw no more the crowded street,
Heard not the tread of hurrying feet—
   I was again a child,

Roaming the wild woods, glad and free,
   Haunting the mountain stream ;
I heard the birds' wild melody,
And through the screen of leaf and tree
   I caught the river's gleam.

The dreamy nook where lilies grew
   I sought by pathways lone,
And where the alder thicket threw
Its tangled shade of dusky hue,
   The snow-white blossoms shone.

And she, that o'er my heart bore rule,
   My sweetheart scarcely ten,
For whose dear sake I stole from school
To pluck the lilies from the pool—
   I see her once again,

As when, upon her desk, my prize
  All sweetly fragrant lay.
The blush that told her glad surprise,
The love-lift of those tender eyes
  Is in my heart to-day.

O Lily fair, with heart of gold !
  Where may thy presence be?
Full many a weary year has rolled
Since, on life's ocean, dark and cold,
  I drifted far from thee.

Perchance, for aught that I may know,
  A staid and sober dame,
She walks this very street.   Ah, no,
My fond heart will not have it so,
  She is to me the same.

And oft, when sleep unseals my eyes,
  With hand in hand again,
We roam beneath unclouded skies
And pluck the flowers of Paradise,
  A boy and girl of ten.
—*1886.*

WILLIAM GARDNER BARTON.

Mr. Barton was born in Salem, Mass., April 4, 1851, and was son of Gardner and Anne Gillis (Donaldson) Barton.   He was educated in the public schools of his native city, leaving the high school in 1869, a few

2

months before the graduation of his class, to take a
clerkship in the Salem National Bank. In 1872 he entered the employ of the First National Bank of Boston,
where he remained until February, 1887, when he resigned his position in order to become cashier for the
Bay State Live Stock Company at Kimball, Cheyenne
county, Nebraska, whither he removed and now resides with his family. This change of location was
made in the hope that the climate of the Western plains
would prove beneficial to his health, which had become
somewhat impaired. Most of his writings have been
contributions to the columns of the *Salem Gazette*, and
have consisted of a few poems, quite a number of essays, and many anonymous book reviews. He seldom
writes now, but a letter from his pen occasionally appears in the *Gazette*. His tastes, being in the line of
natural history, have led him to write mainly upon birds,
trees and natural scenery, and subjects suggested by
his frequent walks in the neighboring town of Beverly,
and in other places. He is a great lover of the writings
of Emerson, Burroughs, Thoreau and Wilson Flagg,
the last two writers having conveyed to him their style
of composition.

JOSHUA'S MOUNTAIN.

The evening robin homeward flies
　To gloaming wood on yonder shore ;
The river smooth in purple lies,
　And sparrow songs come tinkling o'er

From Rial-side, whose verdant mead,
  Still warm from glow of noontime sun,
And pasture where the horses feed,
  And cedars standing one by one,
And forest dark against the sky—
All whisper promise of the eve,
  When nature, moved in rest to feel
How rich the good she doth receive
  In daytime, in her thanks doth kneel.

JAMES BERRY BENSEL.

MR. BENSEL was born in New York City August 2, 1856, and was son of William F. A. and Harriet M. (Berry) Bensel. The family came to Lynn, Mass., when James was in his infancy and the father, becoming insane, died in the Worcester Insane Hospital. The son never married, but took upon himself the care of his mother and his two sisters, and struggled to support himself and them by his literary efforts. His friends became aware of the great burden he was trying to bear and assisted him. Being unsuccessful in Lynn, he finally went to New York City to secure a situation, and took obscure lodgings, in which, soon afterward, at the age of twenty-nine, he died, in sorrow and disappointment, and without friends. The date of his death was February 3, 1886. His disease, which resembled epilepsy, was superinduced by his extreme exertions in endeavoring to earn a living and some fame. In 1883, he published a novel, called "King Cophetna's Wife," as a serial in the *Overland Monthly.* This constituted most of his prose. His poetry, which was worthy of an older brain, was published in the *Boston Transcript,* and other leading newspapers, and in the *Overland Monthly, Atlantic Monthly,* and other magazines, over his full name. Some critics have thought his poetry morbid, and some of it certainly is of that nature. There was very little in his life to make the creations of his mind other than sorrowful; yet at times he wrote as blithely as if he had never known hunger or pain.

His poems were collected in a little volume, entitled "In the King's Garden," and published in 1885. A second edition, with a sketch of the author's life, was published in 1886.

————

MY LITTLE LOVE.

O my little love with the wind-blown hair,
   And the grey eyes full of tears !
You have filled my heart with a grievous care,
   And a weary weight of fears.

O my little love with the tender face !
   You are crueller far to me
Than the mighty wind in its deathly race,
   And crueller than the sea.

For you blow my hopes with your smile or frown
   To life or to death I ween,
And a word from your lips has power to drown
   The light of a day serene.

O my little love whom I hold so dear !
Be kindest of all to me !
Or my life on your love will wreck I fear,
As boats are wrecked by the sea.

ANNE BRADSTREET.

MRS. BRADSTREET was the daughter of Governor Thomas and Dorothy Dudley, and was born at Northampton, in England, in 1612. At the age of sixteen she married Simon Bradstreet, who was afterward the governor of the Massachusetts Bay Colony. Near the time of her marriage she had the small pox, which so reduced her delicate constitution that she became subject to frequent attacks of illness and fits of fainting, and suffered at one time from lameness. Two years later she came to America, with her husband, and lived at Ipswich, Andover and Salem. They had a large family ; and, with her feeble health, her numerous cares, and the burning of her house, in which her books and papers were destroyed, it is remarkable that she wrote at all. Those colonial days, with their dangers, sufferings, severe labors and privations, were far from poetic ; yet she persevered and became celebrated, her poems being commended by Cotton Mather and the witty Ward. The noted John Norton called her "the mirror of her age, and the glory of her sex." She must have had considerable courage to write in those times, when it was thought that mental accomplishments be-

longed exclusively to men.   Perhaps it was enough for
her to know that her husband thought differently, and
that he was proud of her literary attainments.   She was
esteemed for her gracious demeanor and pious conversation, admired for her genius and love of learning, and
honored for her diligence and her wifely and motherly
discretion.   She died at Andover September 16, 1672,
at the age of sixty.   Her husband survived her about a
quarter of a century.

The first edition of Mrs. Bradstreet's poems, entitled
"The Tenth Muse lately sprung up in America, or Several Poems compiled with Great Variety of Wit and
Learning, full of Delight," was published, without her
knowledge, in London, England, in 1650; the second
edition was published in Boston in 1678 ; the third in
1758 ; and the fourth and last in Charlestown in 1867.

————

CONTEMPLATIONS.[1]

Under the cooling shadow of a stately elm,
  Close sate I by a goodly river's side,
Where gliding streams the rocks did overwhelm ;
  A lonely place, with pleasures dignified.
I once that loved the shady woods so well,
Now thought the rivers did the trees excel,
And if the sun would ever shine, there would I dwell.

[1] Extract from "Contemplations," which is acknowledged to be her best
poem.

While on the stealing stream I fixt mine eye,
  Which to the longed-for ocean held its course,
I markt nor crooks nor rubs that there did lie
  Could hinder aught, but still augment its force ;
O happy flood, quoth I, that holdst thy race
Till thou arrive at thy beloved place,
Nor is it rocks or shoals that can obstruct thy pace.

Nor is't enough that thou alone mayst slide,
  But hundred brooks in thy clear waves do meet,
So hand in hand along with thee they glide
  To Thetis' house, where all embrace and greet :
Thou emblem true of what I count the best,
O could I lead my rivulets to rest !
So may we press to that vast mansion, ever blest.

GEORGE JOHNSON BREED.

Mr. Breed was born in Salem, Mass., January 7, 1827, and was son of Capt. Holton J. and Nancy (Symonds) Breed. When he was twenty years of age he went to England to study music, becoming a pupil at the Royal Academy in London. After visiting Germany he returned to America in 1849. He became an accomplished musician, having wonderful skill in the execution of the works of the great masters in the world of harmony and melody. Those who have heard him play will never forget the sweetness and delicacy of his music. Exquisite musical fancies filled his mind, and

he sometimes gave permanent expression to them by
printing his compositions, occasionally publishing songs.
He had a delicate physique, and was remarkable for
the elasticity of his muscular action.   His thought was
deep and alert, and sometimes he seemed so spiritual,
being very absent-minded, that in the circle that knew
him best he was called "Ariel." Being without the care
of a family, having never married, much of his time was
given to reading and to walks in the country, where he
absorbed its natural loveliness.   It is not strange that
such a person should have written poetry, and that of
a high order, though but little was ever published. His
extreme modesty and reserve caused him to withdraw
from society and, known only to a few, pass a secluded
life in his youthful haunts at Salem.   He died of laryn-
gitis, at the Homœopathic Hospital, in Boston, August
12, 1885, at the age of fifty-eight.

SUNSET ON THE ROAD.

I lingered, for it was an hour of heaven !
  I paused, half doubtful might I venture here,
  Where Peace and Glory kissed, dimmed of no tear,—
This blissful rest of love,—*is't freely given?*
All things expectant seemed of some high guest:
  Quiet the cattle stood and mildly gazed,
  As swift his farewell glance in splendor blazed
Across a dreaming world,—and all was blest !
Then nature woke a low-voiced, tranquil hymn,
  The birds outbroke, full-hearted, with a song,

And fields and hills shone bright that had been dim,—
Sure 'tis the *coming* we have waited long !
But lo, the all-seeing eye is slowly hid,
And darkness gathers o'er the closing lid.

———

SUNSET IN THE CITY.

Night gently falls as shade of angel's wing
  Over a world tired in its endless way ;
  Which,—like a child wearied with noisy play
And turning home,—for rest leaves everything.
Divinest hour ! whose stillness wooes to dreams
  Where in the midst of nature—vale and hill,
  River and whispering wood and babbling rill—
Impressed on all sleep's mystic presence seems ;
But *here!*—amid the sad restraints of town,
  The drooping soul no comforter can find ;
And as night's hopeless shade comes settling down,
  Sad thoughts and longings fill both heart and mind ;
Long-buried things awake, memory recalls
The eternal past, till sleep's dark curtain falls.
—*1861.*

————

JONATHAN HUNTINGTON BRIGHT.

Mr. Bright was born in Salem, Mass., where he was baptized by Rev. Thomas Barnard in the North Church July 7, 1802, and was son of Jonathan Bright, an upholsterer of that place. When Jonathan was fifteen years of age, his father died, and he was afterward employed as a clerk in a dry-goods store in his native town. In 1825, he went to Norfolk, Va., where he resided for a while, and about eight years afterward removed to Albany, N. Y. In the autumn of 1836 he sailed to New Orleans, La., and after being there a short time was persuaded to go up the river to Manchester, Miss., a new town, to take part in an important business enterprise. Here he soon contracted the fever of the country by his unwonted privations and exposure to the night air, and after an illness of only a few hours, in that comfortless frontier settlement, away from his family, whom he held most dear, his benignant spirit was delivered up. This was in the month of August, 1837, when he was in his thirty-sixth year. Jones Very calls him, in a memorial poem published a few years after Mr. Bright's decease, "fair Salem's earliest bard." He was a writer of poetry of considerable repute, having regularly contributed to the *Atlantic Souvenir, Williamstown Advocate, Albany Argus, Knickerbocker Magazine*, and other periodicals of his time over the signature of "Viator." He wrote many gems of pure feeling, imbued with the sense of true poetry. The grace, natural simplicity, and beauty of his composition commended itself to every affectionate and sympathizing heart.

NAHANT.

I love thy sea-washed coast, Nahant ! — I love
Thine everlasting cliffs, which tower above ;
I love to linger there when daylight fades,

And evening hangs above her sombre shades,
And lights her pale lamps in the world on high,
 And o'er the rough rocks throws her purple hue ;
  While ocean's heaving tides
  Are beating round thy sides,
 Flinging their foam-wreaths to the sky,
  And flakes of fire seem bursting through
  Each swelling wave of liquid blue !

Tradition lends to thee no hallowed tone ;
Ne'er on thy beach was heard the spirit's moan ;
Yet there's a charm about thee : here I've roved,
In being's blossom, with the forms I loved ;
And they have faded ; many a heart which sprung
Fresh into life when hope and joy were young
Moulders in dust ; and many a buoyant breast,
Which swelled with rapture then, is laid at rest ;
 Many a heart hath met the blight,
 Many an eye is closed in night,
 Many a bosom long may mourn
 For those who never can return !

Each one of us who wanders here,
 And sports within life's little day,
At eve shall sleep upon the bier,
 Our hopes, our promise, passed away :
But thou remain'st ! thy rugged rocks
Shall long withstand time's rudest shocks,
And other feet as light shall tread
Thy wave-bound isle, when we are dead !

Yes, man must bloom and fade, must rise and fall,
Till nature spreads at length o'er earth her pall ;
Then shall thou sink in chaos ! Ay, thy name
Will fall in ruin, and the roll of fame
Shall be a blot ; and the earth, too, and her cherished,
In time's oblivious wreck will all have perished !
—*Aug. 19, 1834.*

CHARLES TIMOTHY BROOKS.

MR. BROOKS was born in Salem, Mass., June 20,
1813, and was son of Timothy and Mary King (Mason)
Brooks. When a boy, his health was delicate, and he
did not participate in boisterous games, delighting instead to roam among the woods and pastures and on
the pebbly beach. He prepared for college at the Latin
Grammar School, and graduated at Harvard in 1832,
and at the divinity school in Cambridge in 1835. He
was ordained over the Unitarian church at Newport,
R. I., June 14, 1837. On account of ill-health he visited the South in 1842, India in 1853, and Europe in
1865. While in Europe, at Stuttgart, he was given a
reception by the German authors on account of his
translations of their works. In 1873, his impaired eye-
sight and other physical infirmities compelled him to
resign his pastorate. He spent the remainder of his life
with his family at Newport, free from care, enjoying his
literary pursuits. He passed gently away June 14, 1883,
lacking six days of three score and ten years. He had

delicate features, was slim in person, of medium height, possessed of attractive manners, and was naturally reverential and pious. He was noted for the purity of his character, gentleness, scholarship, and practical charity. His voice was weak, and his style of preaching was simple and earnest, being almost free from gesture.

Mr. Brooks published thirty-four books, twenty-one of which were translations, chiefly from the German. A translation of Göethe's "Faust" is perhaps the work by which he is best known. His other principal poetical works were three volumes of translated German lyrics, Friedrich Schiller's "Homage to the Arts," a translation, with other poems, Boston, 1846; "Aquidneck, and other Poems," Providence, 1848; and "Songs of Field and Flood," Boston, 1853. A volume of his poems, with a memoir and portrait, was published in Boston in 1885.

———

THE GREAT VOICES.

A voice from the sea to the mountains,
   From the mountains again to the sea ;
A call from the deep to the fountains :
   O spirit ! be glad and be free !

A cry from the floods to the fountains,
   And the torrents repeat the glad song
As they leap from the breast of the mountains :
   O spirit ! be free and be strong !

The pine forests thrill with emotion
Of praise as the spirit sweeps by;
With the voice like the murmur of ocean
To the soul of the listener they cry.

Oh, sing, human heart, like the fountains,
With joy reverential and free;
Contented and calm as the mountains,
And deep as the woods and the sea.
—*Lenox, Aug. 15, 1872.*

WILLIS GAYLORD BURNHAM.

MR. BURNHAM was born in Essex, Mass., January 12, 1846, and was son of Samuel and Sarah (Andrews) Burnham. A bachelor, he has always lived with his parents at his birthplace, in a quiet, uneventful manner. Here he has enjoyed many of his leisure hours in reading and occasionally writing for the local newspapers, his contributions being principally poetry. From his earliest years, he has been a lover of the water. Nature in all its changes gives him pleasure; spring being his favorite season. Birds and flowers, and all that true poets love are dear to him. Books have been his constant companions, especially those devoted to history; and art of all kinds gives him much entertainment. He inherited his poetic talent from his mother, who was herself no mean writer. His poetry is pretty and is liked. His temperament is genial and pleasant; and he is happy and contented with the quiet life, which was so desirable to his widowed mother, whose declining years he made enjoyable by his filial care and affection. Though now a local poet, he will be better known, and his poetry still more appreciated by and by, when a volume of his verses shall have been collected and published. His home is pleasantly situated; and from the windows of his residence a beautiful landscape, varied with river, field and wood, and in the distance an ocean view, presents itself. Here he can continue to dream his dreams, and write them out that other minds may enjoy the happy musings of his own.

———

THE LITTLE ONES GONE HOME.

There are three little darlings
    Watching for me,
On the beautiful shore,
    By the stormless sea.
And the light of their smiles,
    In that bright realm afar,
Seems to shed on my soul
    Through the portals ajar.

I think of them most
    When the morning is nigh,
And the night clouds grow bright
    On the clear eastern sky;
For my visions are then
    Of that blest other side,
Of the radiant dawn
    O'er the darksome tide.

As they play amid flowers
　Surpassingly fair,—
My darlings ! my darlings !
　I see them all there ;
Happy while waiting
　And watching for me,
On the beautiful shore
　By the stormless sea.

WILLIAM WARNER CALDWELL.

MR. CALDWELL was born in Newburyport, Mass.,
October 28, 1823, and was son of John and Eleanor
(Orne) Caldwell. He attended Dummer Academy,
under the preceptorship of Professor Cleaveland, from
1833 to 1839, when he entered Bowdoin College, from
which he graduated in 1843. In 1845, he entered business as a druggist in his native place, and remained
there in the business until 1881, when he disposed of
his establishment and retired. Since then he has resided in Boston and vicinity, devoting much of his time
to literary pursuits. His poems have been received
with great favor and admiration for their purity, grace
and tenderness. His occasional verses on simple, heart-
felt themes are truthful in expression and sentiment, and
happy in poetic execution. Whittier said of him, that
he was the best lyric poet in New England. He has
also won a good reputation by his numerous translations from the German poets, Gribel, Hebel, Fallersle-

ben, and others. "The Watchman's Cry," from Hebel,
is one of the many German gems that he has made fa-
miliar to English readers. More than fifty of his German lyric translations have been set to music by John
W. Tufts for the "Normal Music Course." He is a
man of refinement and cultivated tastes. He was married, in 1848, to Miss Ruth M. Woodcock, a lady of
Leicester, Mass., to whom the poem given below is addressed.

In 1857, Mr. Caldwell published a volume of poetry,
entitled "Poems, Original and Translated."

BY THE RIVER.

TO R. M. C.

From mountain peak and village spire
　　The golden sunlight fades away,
But up the clear sky, high and higher,
　　With deepening radiance, doth ray
　　The glory of the dying day,
In streams of rosy-gleaming fire.

Upon the river's marge I stand,
　　And gaze across the shadowy blue,
As, rippling up the shelving strand,
　　The mimic waves their foam-bells strew,
　　Slide softly back, then come anew,
And murmur up the glistening sand.

3

How sweet to feel this dewy air
   Blow freshly o'er the unruffled tide !
So tenderly it lifts my hair,
   So wooes the modest flowers that hide
   Their little cups, anear my side,
To greet me with their perfume rare.

And sweet it is, at times, to hear
   The dip of oars, the lingering sweep,
As some light boat its course doth steer
   Towards the far-off billowy deep,
   So falls the measured chime they keep,
With silvery cadence on the ear.

And look ! above yon monarch pine,
   That sentinels the distant shore,
Our chosen star doth brightly shine,
   And, all the charméd waters o'er,
   Her pure and lustrous light doth pour,
Recalling thee and hopes divine.

I would thou wert beside me now,
   Beneath this gnarléd beechen tree,
To watch the river's placid flow,
   And hear the wavelets gurgling glee,
   As on the lone shore, merrily,
Unceasingly they come and go,—

That I might gaze upon thy face,
   Drink gladness from thy loving eyes,

And feel again the wondrous grace,
That in thy every action lies ;
Or speak and hear thy low replies,
Or hold thee in my close embrace.

Vain wish.   But wheresoe'er to-night,
Or far or near thy footsteps rove,
When yon dear star shall meet thy sight,
Oh ! may its welcome radiance move
Thy gentle heart to dreams of love,
And bring thee peace and calm delight.

JOHN WHITE CHADWICK.

MR. CHADWICK was born in Marblehead, Mass., October 19, 1840, and was son of John White and Jane
(Stanley) Chadwick. Leaving school at the age of thirteen, he worked for some months in a dry-goods store,
and afterward engaged in shoe-making until he was
seventeen years old, when he entered the Bridgewater
Normal School, from which he graduated in 1859.
Shortly afterward, he went to the academy at Exeter,
N. H., and after studying there, and with a private tutor for a year, entered the Cambridge divinity school,
from which he graduated in 1864. He was ordained
over the Second Unitarian church in Brooklyn, N. Y.,
December 21, 1864, and still remains there. He has
contributed articles to the *Christian Examiner, The
Radical, Old and New, Harper's Magazine,* and various other publications. He has also written numerous

poems, book reviews, and other productions for the
*Christian Register, Liberal Christian, Independent, and
Christian Union.* His poems are characterized by a
rare beauty and tenderness, and have found a loving reception in many hearts. They have fulfilled the rich
promise of his early efforts, growing richer, deeper,
fuller of the poetic fervency of his mind. He is one
of the prominent hymn writers of the liberal faith, his
songs being admired by the Unitarians and others of
the more liberal religious denominations, and no less
acceptable to those who, though proclaiming themselves to be stricter in doctrine, have the spirit of truth
and a love for God.

SEALED ORDERS.

Our life is like a ship that sails some day
To distant waters leagues on leagues away;
Not knowing what command to do and dare
Awaits her when her eager keel is there.

Birth, Love, and Death are ports we leave behind,
Borne on by rolling wave and rushing wind;
Bearing a message with unbroken seal,
Whose meaning fain we would at once reveal.

And there are friends that stand upon the shore,
And watch our sail till it is seen no more,
And cry, "Oh, would that we might know the way
The brave ship goes for many a weary day!"

It may not be.   But ever and anon
Some order, sealed at first, we ope and con ;
So learn what next, so east or westward fly,
And ne'er again that port of Birth espy.

How many another craft goes dancing by !
What pennants float from morn and evening sky !
By day how white our wake behind us streams !
By night what golden phosphorescent gleams !

There comes a day when Love, that lies asleep
The fairest island in the mighty deep,
Wakes on our sight.   Its fragrant shores we reach,
And grates our keel upon its shining beach.

There do we stay awhile ; but soon again
We trim our sails to seek the open main ;
And now, whatever winds and waves betide,
Two friendly ships are sailing side by side.

Where lies their course in vain they seek to know,
" Go forth, " the Spirit says, and forth they go ;
Enough that, wherever they may fare,
Alike the sunshine and the storm they share.

Islands that none e'er visited before
Invite to land with easy shelving shore ;
Circes and sirens fling their challenge out,
Charybdis deafens Scylla's deafening shout.

For still these ships keep joyful company,
And many new strange lands they haste to see.
In port of Love 'twas pleasant to abide,
But oh ! Love's sea is very deep and wide.

Ay, deep and wide, and yet there comes a day
When these fond ships must sail a parted way ;
The port of Death doth one of them beguile,
The other lingers for a little while.

Lingers as near as she may dare to go,
And plies the cold, gray offing to and fro ;
Waiting impatient for the high command
To sail into the shadow of the land.

Is this the end ? I know it cannot be.
Our ships shall sail upon another sea ;
New islands yet shall break upon our sight,
New continents of love and truth and might.

But still not knowing, still with orders sealed,
Our track shall lie across the heavenly field ;
Yet there, as here, though dim the distant way,
Our strength shall be according to our day.

The sea is His, He made it, and His grace
Lurks in its wildest wave, its deepest place :
Our truest knowledge is that He is wise ;
What is our foresight to His sweet surprise ?

JOSEPH WARREN CHAPMAN.

MR. CHAPMAN was born in Marblehead, Mass., November 26, 1855, and was son of Joseph Warren and Louisa (Morse) Chapman. He fitted for college in the high school of his native town, and graduated at Dartmouth in 1879, being the author of the class ode. He has devoted his life to school teaching, having taught at Billerica, been sub-master of Dean Academy, in Franklin, Mass., principal of Lincoln Academy, at Lincoln, Va., and principal of the Marblehead high school. He has taught in the latter school for the last six years, and still pursues his work there. He resides in Marblehead, and has a family. He is a well-read man; and has taught literature to private students, having at present a class in Browning, in reference to which his sonnet, entitled "Fellowship," was written. He has also read lectures on several authors; and has contributed poems to the *Wheelman* (the magazine now called *Outing*), and to the *Boston Courier*, *Boston Transcript*, and local newspapers.

———

FELLOWSHIP.

Sweet friends are mine,—I never walk alone,—
Though all unseen by you they go along,
The loving ghosts from out the realm of song,
With gleeful laugh, or, haply, making moan.

For me the rose is never over-blown,
The sparrow mute, though winter tarries long ;
More truly living round my pathway throng
These birdlike guests from other ages flown.
They know not death, for they are heavenly born.
I love them all ; I weep with them, I laugh,
They give my soul of Eunoe's rill to quaff, —
Helen of Troy ; old Timon clad in scorn ;
And others many.   Hark ! upon the wind,
From Arden blown, the mock of Rosalind.

—

AN EPITAPH.

Say not that he who lies below is dead,
But rather, he we loved was wont to wear
A garb of flesh, bedecked with joy and care,
And with the nerves of motion fashionéd ;
And fondly say, one day he donned instead
A robe befitting courts supremely fair
And God's high presence ; nothing could compare
Of earthly glory with it ; and that he said :
"Weep not, dear friends, that now I go away,
For ye will follow soon ; in some pure sphere
We'll meet to joy again."   So smiling say,
The garment that he wore is lying here ;
But he, as birds the summer sometime lent,
Hath left us lone, grieving, yet half content.

HENRY HENDERSON CLARK.

MR. CLARK was born in Georgetown, Mass., April 1, 1831, and was son of Aaron Lufkin and Mary (Adams) Clark. He was an exceedingly bright and intelligent lad, and a good scholar, receiving his education in the public schools of his native town, and academies in Salisbury, N. H., Brownington, Vt., and Bridgton, Maine. He learned the trade of a printer in Haverhill, Mass., and began work as a journeyman compositor in the University Press office at Cambridge, becoming final proof reader, and then manager of its fine book department. After being there thirty years he resigned and took charge of Rand, Avery & Co's book department in Boston, where four years afterward he established an office of his own, turning out work second to none in quality. He was the intimate acquaintance of Longfellow, Greeley, Lowell, Sumner, Agassiz, and many other lettered men. Mr. Clark was endowed with rare literary talents, and was refined, sensitive and pureminded. He loved nature passionately, and his writings breathe of the country, its birds and flowers, its hills and valleys, rivers and brooks. He wrote mainly over the signature of "Henry Henderson," many of his poems having been written for the *Boston Transcript*. He lived in Cambridge during the thirty years he was employed by the University Press, then in Melrose, and a year or two later removed to Malden, where his family still reside. After an illness of three weeks, terminating a decline of several years, he died at Malden April 15, 1888, at the age of fifty-seven.

PARKER RIVER.

Through broad gleaming meadows of billowy grass,
That form at its outlet a long narrow pass,
  The river comes down,
By farms whose high tillage gives note to the town,
  As sparkling and bright
  As it gladdened the sight
Of the fathers who first found its beautiful shore,
And felt here was home,—they need wander no more.

When the swallows were gathering in flocks for their
    flight,
As if conscious some foe of their kind were in sight,
  They pushed up the stream
In the low level rays of the sun's lingering beam,
  That lit all below
  With a magical glow,
That brought by resemblance old England to mind,
Whose shores they had left with such heartache behind.

The golden-rod waved its tall plumes from the bank,
As if the whole bright summer sunshine it drank ;
  And grapes full and fair
Their wild native fragrance flung out on the air ;
  And asters, and all
  The gay flowerets of fall,
That brighten the season's long dreamy delight,
Were crowding the woodside their beauty made bright.

In the soft sunny days of September they came,
When the trees here and there were alight with the flame
  That betokens decay,

And the passing of summer in glory away ;
     As if the great Cause
     Of nature's grand laws
Had set his red signet that here should be stayed
The tide of the year in its pomp and parade.

And now, as I stand on this broad open height,
And take in the view with enraptured delight,
     I feel as they felt
Who in fervor of soul by these bright waters knelt,
     That here I could rest
     In the consciousness blest
That nature has given all heart, hand or eye
Could crave for contentment that earth can supply ;—

The limitless ocean that stretches away
Beyond the bright islets that light up the bay,
     The murmurous roar
Of the surf breaking in on the long line of shore,
     And rivers that run
     Like gold in the sun,
And broad sunny hillsides and bright breezy groves,
And all one instinctively longs for and loves.

Trees bending with fruit touched with tints of the morn,
Fields soft with the late springing verdure unshorn,
     And glimpses so fair
Of city and river and sails here and there,
     And cottages white
     On the beach by the light,
The picturesque roadside, and vistas that seem
Like openings to fairy-land seen but in dream.

O, well may old Newbury be proud of its soil,
That brings such return for the laborer's toil;
> But proudest of all
Of the men whose achievements she loves to recall,
> Who sprung from the few
> Of the lone shallop's crew
Who two centuries ago, creeping Plum Island Sound,
This stream in the heart of the wilderness found.

In yonder old churchyard the forefathers sleep
Whose moss-covered headstones the bright record keep,
> In rude rustic rhyme,
Or the quaint, honest phrase of "ye oldene tyme,"
> Of all they went through
> The rough earth to subdue,
And plant for their kindred and all who may come
The broad, firm foundations of freedom's proud home.

At thy source, silent river, in childhood I played,
And followed thy windings through sunshine and shade,
> As joyous and free
As thy own light and soft tripping down to the sea;
> And thoughtful I stand
> And look in on the land
To the hills that in glory flash out in the sun,
Where life in these sweet dreamy vales was begun.

Here Parker the elder, who gave thee his name,
And coupled his own with thy pastoral fame,
> Stood out at the head

Of the brave little band he so lovingly led,
    To seek and to find
    The wealth of earth mined
By Faith, Toil and Patience,—the handmaids of Skill,
That wait to obey the stern mandates of Will.

Thou stream by the stranger unsought and unknown,
That into my heart like an old friend hast grown,
    For all the glad hours
I have rambled with thee through thy bright happy
    bowers,
    I would bring the best gift
    To thee I could lift,
In happy remembrance of dear old days gone,
Whose joy in my heart like a dream will live on.

Adieu, gentle river ! Long, long may I wait
Ere here I stand in the day's golden gate,
    And take in the view
That brings back the past as so old and so new ;
    But memory will still
    Haunt this storied old hill
Whence I see as in vision the prospect unrolled
In all the bright splendor of purple and gold.
—*1878.*

ROBERT STEVENSON COFFIN.

Mr. Coffin was born in Brunswick, Me., July 14,
1794, and was son of Rev. Ebenezer and Mary Coffin.
The family removed to Newburyport, Mass., in 1802,

and a few years later Robert was apprenticed to a printer. During the war of 1812, he was a sailor, and for a time a prisoner on board an English frigate. He soon afterward obtained employment at his trade in a newspaper office in Boston, where he worked until 1818, when he went to New York City, arriving there a destitute stranger. After some time he secured a job, on which he worked about eight months, and occasionally wrote for a small periodical over the *nom de plume* of "Albert." Philadelphia being more liberally disposed toward native talent, he went there, and obtained a situation in a daily-journal printing office. While there he adopted the appellation of "Boston Bard," and three years later his poems found their way into British papers. He was then employed as assistant-editor of the *Independent Balance* until the publisher died ; and afterward wrote and worked for the *Saturday Evening Post*, having in the meantime married. He travelled back to New York, intemperate and without money, and, stopping in Yorktown, with a Quaker family, wrote for several public journals. Having been sick with consumption for three years, he desired to see his old home once more, started on his way thither, and died at Rowley, Mass., May 7, 1827, at the age of thirty-two.

Mr. Coffin published two volumes of poetry,—"The Printer, and Several Other Poems," in 1817 ; and the "Oriental Harp ; Poems of the Boston Bard," with his portrait, in 1826.

His "Life," written by himself, was published in 1825.

MELANCHOLY.

She dwells by the stream where the cypress and willow,
  Are gemmed with the tears that fall from her eye;
The earth is her bed and the flint-stone her pillow,
  Midnight her mantle, her curtain the sky.

Her cell is the cave, where the bright beam of morning
  Ne'er pierced the chill gloom of its wildering maze,
Where the sun-shine of joy, youth's visage adorning,
  Ne'er warmed with its fire, or cheered with its rays.

The moon is her lamp, when the mist-mantled mountain
  She clambers at midnight and walks o'er its steep:
Or leans on a rock of a crystalline fountain,
  And sighs to the tempest that howls o'er the deep.

Her tresses are dark as the wing of the raven,
  Her robes are all wet, and her bosom is bare;
Like a barque on the waves, 'mid the whirlwinds of
      heaven,
  She wanders distracted, or sinks in despair.
—*1817.*

ABEL GARDNER COURTIS.

Mr. Courtis was born in Lynn, Mass., March 29, 1838, and was son of Benjamin and Rebecca (Harris) Courtis, whose ancestors have been for generations natives of the county. He was educated in the common schools of his native place; and, in the office of the *Lynn Bay State*, in his teens, he learned the art of print-

ing. In 1856, he went on a whaling voyage to the
Okhotsk Sea, and was gone two years. After his return,
he worked at his trade in Boston, and became foreman
of the office of the *Lynn Reporter*, continuing in that
capacity five years. In 1867, a good field for a new
journal appearing in Lynn, Mr. Courtis, with two other
gentlemen, founded the *Lynn Transcript*, of which he
was one of the conductors until 1877, when he became
sole conductor and proprietor. In 1881, he sold the
office and the paper, and since that time has been engaged in the business of book-binding in Lynn. He
married in 1859, and settled in his native place, where
he has since resided. Most of Mr. Courtis' literary work
has been done for his paper. In quantity he has produced the least verse of any of the Essex county poets·
Besides the sonnet, which follows this sketch, another,
entitled "Our Heritage," appearing in the introductory
portion of this volume, is from his pen. Mr. Courtis is
an enthusiastic lover of nature, and is also interested in
the progress of the mechanic arts, and in questions of
metaphysics, the relations of science and religion, and
kindred subjects that so much engage modern thought.

———

TO THE SEA.

Thy storm-wrought surges, O majestic Sea !
   Assail the solid continents, and shake
Their foam-crests to the gale, in jubilee
   Of thy stupendous energies, that wake
   Whene'er the winds—thy chosen allies—take

The mandate of the sun, their forces grand
To link with thine in elemental glee !
E'en in thy moods of calm, when on the strand
Thy lighter pulses beat in wanton play,
   The impress of sublimity and power—
Of force reserved—forever marks thy way.
   From an Almighty hand the primal dower
Of grandeur, strength and beauty came to thee—
Unchanging emblem thou of vast eternity !
—*November, 1888.*

———

STEPHEN PIERSON DRIVER.

Mr. Driver was born in Salem, Mass., December 20, 1829, and was son of Stephen and Mary (Beckford) Driver. His early years were spent in his native place, where he graduated from the high school. He became a partner with his father in the manufacture of ladies' boots and shoes ; and on his father's retirement from business, in connection with his brothers, he carried on the business at Lynn. He sold out, and, with others, fitted up a ware-room under the Globe Theatre in Boston as New England agents for the Weber piano. Later he became a life-insurance agent, and, subsequently, was agent for Charles Scribner's Sons, publishers, of New York, whom he still represents. As to his literary attainment, that which he has produced has, so to speak, largely written itself. He has been a contributor to many of the leading papers, a large number of his po-

4

ems having been occasional and local, and most of
them outgrowths of the times. Early in the Rebellion
he entered the service on the non-commissioned staff of
the twenty-third Massachusetts Regiment, and remained
in the army about two years in North Carolina. He then
held a civil office in the State Department there. He
was for some years secretary of the Salem Moral Society
and was also for several years a member of the Salem
city government. He has always been actively interested in musical matters in Salem and in Lowell, his
present place of residence. He was president of "The
Amphions" in Salem, held an office in the Salem Choral
Society, and has been choir-master in many churches in
Salem and Lowell. Since removing to Lowell, he has
been leader of the Hatton Club, and organizer and
leader of the Amphion Male Chorus, and the Madrigal
Club.

THE EMPTY SHOES.

Oh, blessed trust ! whatever else betide
God's gates of gold are ever opened wide
When infant feet press up the other side.

    .   .   .   .   .

Only two little shoes !
Two tiny, smooth-worn shoes,
With my best treasures laid aside,
But, never from my heart away,
By night or day,
Since Baby died.

Two little, tear-wet shoes !
And yet I can't refuse
The lessons they teach to my spirit-ear ;
I can but hear
The messages of love they bring,
The words of hope they utter near,
The echoed songs they sing.

They whisper to me of our sundered bond,
Of the Vale of Dark, and the light Beyond ;
Of the kind, strong hand,
That our darling led
Through the silent pathways of the dead,
To the Better Land.

They tell me of earthly paths untrod ;
They lead me up to the streets of God ;
And they show me the gate where she passed in,
Her garments unstained by the soil of sin ;
And, as I sit in this shrouded room,
They scatter the gloom,
And the night is aglow with light and bloom.

Oh, wee, worn shoes ! ye are richer to me
Than are gold and gems of mine and sea !
For the bliss ye speak is not bought and sold—
More priceless than gems, more enduring than gold—
And her sandals of joy can never grow old,
The sandals, love-wrought, which her feet infold.

Oh, the dainty, dimpled feet !
Cherub-feet, with glory shod,

On the street
Paved with pearl and amethyst,
Where they ramble, as they list,
Up and down the radiant highways,
Through the music-haunted by-ways,
By the thronging angels trod,
In the city called the Beautiful—the paradise of God.

Oh, the waiting little feet !
Safe, within the sure retreat,
Safe, so near the mercy-seat ;
They shall wander ne'er again
On the slippery slopes of Pain,
Never grope, nor tire, nor stumble in earth's darkness
or its rain.

Safe for aye, from sin and sorrow,
Till the dawn of some to-morrow,
When, adown the heavenly street,
We shall greet
The on-coming of the welcome, and the patter of the
feet.

MARTHA LUCINDA EMERSON.

Mrs. Emerson was born in Chelmsford, Mass., November 1, 1832, and was daughter of Rev. John and
Celia (Burrows) Parkhurst. She was one of eleven children. Her father was a clergyman of the Baptist denomination, with a small salary and a large farm, on
which the children found employment and a happy

childhood. Mattie attended the district and private schools, and also spent several terms at the academy. At the age of ten, she united with her father's church. Two years later a dissension occurred in the church, and she, with about one half of the members, asked for and obtained a dismissal. Those who had left formed a new church, which Mattie refused to join. Doubts arose in her mind as to the consistency of the Baptist faith, and at length she adopted a belief resembling Spiritualism. She says : "Since then the light has steadily increased, the darkness of the misty man-made creeds disappearing like frostwork before the sun, until I feel that I stand in the glorious light and liberty of the children of the one eternal God." She married Mr. Rufus W. Emerson of Chelmsford in 1855, and has resided for twenty years in Boxford. As a child she was imaginative and spent a large portion of her time in happy day-dreams, but since her marriage, has devoted herself almost exclusively to the active duties of domestic life. Her children were married several years ago, so she is again giving much of her time to the society of the muse, of whom she has learned so well. She has published about two hundred articles in the local newspapers. Her health is poor and her hair has begun to turn gray, but she is as genial and spiritualistic as ever.

A PICTURE.

A storm-dark night, and sky
Where clouds wind-driven fly,

Their jagged outlines by sharp lightnings gilt ;
   Roaring of crested surge
   Which gales tempestuous urge
On rocks, like castles by the Titans built.

   One rock rose black and bare
   In the spray-moistened air,
And all around it dread abysses yawned ;
   And on its summit stood
   In fearful solitude,
One with a face as though the day had dawned.

   With eyes upturned he gazed,
   A steady hand upraised,
Pointing to where through parted clouds were seen
   A planet's radiant eye
   Looking serene and high
In peaceful faith upon the awful scene.

   Lift up thy voice, O sea !
   Chant of the mystery
That thy unfathomed depths hold evermore !
   Dash thy wild waves on high
   Towards the wild threatening sky,
Time's breaking chords shall catch thy final roar !

   But the enraptured eyes,
   Lifted to opening skies,
On glorious down-pouring light are placed ;
   Life's terrors cannot harm,
   Her faith's eternal calm
Rears a firm rock amidst the howling waste.

SAMUEL WALTER FOSS.

Mr. Foss was born in Candia, N. H., June 19, 1858, and was son of Dyer and Polly (Hardy) Foss. He graduated from the Portsmouth, N. H., high school in 1877, and from Brown University in 1882, being poet of his class. He settled in Lynn, Mass., and became sole editor and manager of the *Lynn Saturday Union* in 1883. He continued in that position until 1886, when the paper was sold. He then became a regular contributor to the *Boston Globe, New York Sun, Puck, The Judge, Time, Detroit Free Press*, and *Tid Bits*, and an occasional writer for *The Yankee Blade, New York World, Chicago Ledger, Lynn Saturday Union*, and other publications. In August, 1887, he became editor of *The Yankee Blade*, a position which he still holds. He has done much editorial work for daily papers, and many of the best articles found in the editorial columns of some of the Boston dailies were from his pen. He was sometimes called by *Tid Bits*, "Our Own Poet," and wrote a page or so each week for it, mostly anonymously. He has generally signed his articles, " S. W. Foss," sometimes with his initials, and in a few instances, " F. S. Walters." While editor of the *Union* he originated the so-called " long-tailed " style of versification. Mr. Foss has written some good serious poems, but the great mass of his work has been of the comic class. In this he has been very successful, having furnished to the public some of the best hits and satires ever published. The name of " Sam Foss " is

known to the readers of the leading publications devoted to humorous literature the world over.

NATURE'S CALL FOR MEN.

Bring me men to match my mountains,
 Bring me men to match my plains,
Clear of heart as woodland fountains,
 With new eras in their brains.
Bring me men of native power,
 Trained and magnified by art,
Bring me men whose richest dower
 Is their rectitude of heart.

Bring me men of lofty vision,
 Bring me men of hopeful cheer,
Men of high and proud derision—
 Bring me men who mock at fear ;
Bring me men of strong emotions,
 Men of natures quick and warm,
Men with heart-throbs like the ocean's
 In the tempest and the storm.

Bring me men of proud defiance,
 Bring me men of righteous hate,
Bring me young and thoughtful giants,
 Strong to bear the blows of fate.
Bring me men of sacred passion,
 Bring me men of holy rage,
Men whose fiery thought shall fashion,
 Guide and sanctify their age.

Bring me men of fervid gladness,
  Bring me men whose hearts attune
To the glad and sportive madness
  Of the singing birds of June.
Men of laughter like a fountain,
  Men whose gladness cheer shall be,
Like the moonlight on the mountain,
  Or the sunlight on the sea.

Bring me men whose lofty mission
  Is the world's work, yet unwrought,
Men of glad prophetic vision,
  Men of grand and bard-like thought—
Bring me men to match my mountains,
  Bring me men to match my plains,
Clear of heart as woodland fountains,
  With new eras in their brains.

WILLIAM LLOYD GARRISON.

MR. GARRISON was born in Newburyport, Mass., December 10, 1805, and was son of Capt. Abijah and Frances Maria (Lloyd) Garrison. Becoming a printer quite young, the office was his teacher. He edited *The Free Press,* and afterward *The National Philanthropist.* He became the slave's advocate ; and, connecting himself with *The Genius of Universal Emancipation,* in a voice of thunder he demanded their immediate freedom. In 1831, he founded *The Liberator*, which lived till the bondmen became free, being first published in a dark chamber in Boston, by the help of a negro boy. The apathy of the clergy on the slave question caused a change from his Orthodox belief to a liberal faith: he was no infidel, as is sometimes said. He made three trips to Great Britain to stir up the anti-slavery interest there. In 1835, in Boston, he was mobbed and dragged through the street, his clothing being torn from his person. Full of courage and faith in God he pushed forward till the cause triumphed, and then retired to private life. Going to Great Britain in 1867 on account of ill-health, a public breakfast was held in his honor in London, a dinner at Manchester, suppers at Newcastle-on-Tyne, Edinburgh and Glasgow; and the freedom of Edinburgh was given to him. He afterward lived quietly at "Rockledge" in Roxbury, Mass., and, after a distressing illness, died in New York City May 24, 1879, at the age of seventy-three. His style of speaking and writing was simple. He was not an orator; but his intense earnestness gave him the attention and sympathy of his audiences. He was genial and modest, thinking little of himself, but everything of his cause. He wrote poetry throughout his marvellous career, and some of his sonnets are hardly excelled in depth of feeling and poetic beauty.

His poems have been published in a volume.

Two memoirs of him, with portraits and other engravings, were published, one in 1880 and the other in two volumes in 1885.

LIBERTY FOR ALL.

They tell me, Liberty ! that in thy name
  I may not plead for all the human race,
  That some are born to bondage and disgrace,
So, to a heritage of woe and shame,
And some to power supreme, and glorious fame :
  With my whole soul I spurn the doctrine base
  And, as an equal brotherhood, embrace
All people, and for all fair freedom claim !
Know this, O man ! whate'er thy earthly fate—
  God never made a tyrant nor a slave :
Woe, then, to those who dare to desecrate
  His glorious image—for to all He gave
Eternal rights which none may violate ;
  And by a mighty hand, th' oppressed He yet shall
    save !
  ___

FREEDOM OF THE MIND.[1]

High walls and huge the body may confine,
  And iron grates obstruct the prisoner's gaze,
And massive bolts may baffle his design,
  And vigilant keepers watch his devious ways :
Yet scorns th' immortal mind this base control !
  No chains can bind it and no cell inclose :
Swifter than light, it flies from pole to pole,
  And, in a flash, from earth to heaven it goes !
It leaps from mount to mount—from vale to vale
  It wanders, plucking honeyed fruits and flowers ;

[1] This sonnet was written on the wall of his cell while imprisoned for libel.

It visits home, to hear the fireside tale,
  Or in sweet converse pass the joyous hours :
'Tis up before the sun, roaming afar,
And, in its watches, wearies every star !

EMILY ADAMS GETCHELL.

MISS GETCHELL was born in Newbury, now a part of
Newburyport, Mass., February 7, 1850, and was daughter of Hubbard and Hannah Rolfe (Pillsbury) Getchell.
She is of pure Yankee ancestry, which she betrays in
her ingenious poems and witticisms. She was educated
at the Putnam Free School, and has resided ever since
her birth in the house in which she was born. She has
always been interested in literature, and began to compose verses when she was but eight years of age, though
she did not appear in print until her eighteenth year.
She has published her contributions to the press over the
nom de plumes of " Clephane Ritchie " and " Collette,"
and has written for the *Newburyport Herald, Waverly
Magazine, Ballou's Monthly Magazine,* and other periodicals in Boston and Augusta. Her writings betray
an apprehensive and thoroughly read mind, an interest
in history, and a due appreciation of the minor lines
which make up the perfectness of a pen picture. She
is one of the few now resident in the county, who are
worthy to take a place among the gifted with this heav-
en-born talent. She is of medium height, slender in

figure, and a blonde, with a nervous temperament, her mental powers being stronger than her physical. She has strong perseverance and will power, and large musical and artistic faculties. She mingles in society, and takes her part in public affairs, being prominently connected with several organizations, charitable, literary and social.

———

FROBISHER——DAVIS——GREELEY.

" WAES HEIL !"

It—*i. e.* the discovery of the northwest passage or the north pole—is still the only thing left undone, whereby a notable mind might be made famous and remarkable.—*Martin Frobisher,* 16*th century.*

The sea-birds wheel above the cliffs of Devon,
  The summer sun beats down
On fisher's boats all idle, and beyond them
  The brown roofs of the town.

High festival the hearty folk are keeping—
  Unchecked the mirth and din ;
And young and old press round the low-browed portal
  And windows of the inn,

To scan, if haply fortune bless their vision,
  With pride those stalwart forms
And faces tanned, grown stern in many a battle
  With northern ice and storms.

Happy the eager ears that catch the burden
  Of wondrous stories told
Of awesome sounds, foul vapors, and the deadly
  White terror of the cold ;

How when the grizzly death his icy fingers
  Laid on their comrades brave,
Amid the eternal snows, in the grim midnight,
  They made their lonely grave.

When perils past and safely at their haven
  With joy their hearts were stirred,
Their royal mistress for their toils and daring,
  Thanked them with gracious word.

The tankards brimming o'er with generous liquor
  Circle from hand to hand ;
Staunch loyal Britons all, they shout together
  For queen and native land.

"*Waes heil! waes heil!* ye sea-dogs of bold Devon !"
  The pledge rings far and free ;
The startled gulls and curlews scream an echo
  Over the white-capped sea.

The days and years sink down time's silent ocean
  Till centuries are told ;
But hero hearts and deeds know of no nation,
  Their spirit ne'er grows old.

The sea-kings stout, brave Frobisher and Davis,
  Are dust and ashes all ;

The Tudor lioness sleeps at Westminster
  Beneath her velvet pall ;

But the glad voice of greeting and of triumph
  Still sounds across the tide ;
A sister-land brings home her sea-worn heroes
  With joy and love and pride.

Still thy unquiet waves to bear them over,
  O, leaping harbor bar !
Sing "Home, sweet home," O, yellow shifting sand dunes,
  And Newbury's hills afar.

Crowd the long, shaded streets and hang out banners,
  Rouse up the ancient town ;
For sires and grandsires see their age fall from them
  With every child's renown.

Open the doors alike to son and stranger,
  Make broad the board within,
For joy, like sorrow, levels prince and peasant,
  And makes the whole world kin.

Would God we had them all ! Pitiless kingdom
  Of the eternal frost,
Thou guardest secrets well ; we read thy archives
  At what a bitter cost.

Not all unmixed the laurel and the oak-leaf,
  Droops forth the cypress, too ;
We crown ye with DeLong, and Hall and Franklin,
  O, gallant hearts and true !

Peace to their ashes ! Their life duties ended,
    God giveth them His sleep,
Hail to the living, rescuers and rescued,
    Their fame we green will keep.

Safe home at last ! The eyes that gaze are misty,
    And words grow poor and fail ;
We fill the loving-cup to over-flowing—
    Brothers and friends, "*Waes heil!*"

NOTE. "*Waes heil !*" is an old Norse drinking salutation,
meaning, literally, "Be in health." The English synonym is,
"Here's to you!" or "I'll pledge you!" Martin Frobisher made
voyages to the polar regions 1576–1578. John Davis made his
most noteworthy voyages in the same direction 1585–1588. Lt.
Greeley arrived at his home in Newburyport in 1884, and this
poem was written for and read at his reception.

HANNAH FLAGG GOULD.

MISS GOULD was born in Lancaster, Mass., September 3, 1789, and was daughter of Capt. Benjamin and Grizzel Apthorp (Flagg) Gould. She never married, and resided with her father, at first in her native town, soon afterward removing with him to Newburyport, where the remainder of her life was spent. She found her chief joy in being the solace of her father's declining years. She was his sole companion ; and her unceasing care, tender solicitude, and delightful temperament cheered his weary loneliness as long as his spirit could be kept from the confines of the other world. After

his decease, she continued to write verses, as she had
done for several years, in her graceful and playful style.
Her poems have always been much admired.   Her
tone is often tender, and the lyrics she composed are
of a simple, easy cast, being pervaded by her gentle and
pure spirit, and having within them a charming rhythm,
which gave them a permanency in the memory.   She
was vivacious and witty, and wrote but little of love,
seemingly giving but little thought to the subject.   In
Newburyport, September 5, 1865, at the age of seventy-
six, she departed, as she had herself written, to

> "That country, that home, the unsatisfied spirit
> Here sighs to recover, and hopes to inherit."

Her name will always be held in affectionate remembrance for her disinterested and devoted love to her
aged father, as well as for the artless beauty and sweetness of her writings.

Beside her prose writings, Miss Gould published, in
verse, "The Diosma" in 1850 ; "The Youth's Coronal"
in 1851 ; " Hymns and Poems for Children " in 1854 ;
and general collections in 1832, 1835, 1841, and in
1850.

A NAME IN THE SAND.

Alone I walked the ocean strand ;
A pearly shell was in my hand ;
I stooped and wrote upon the sand
    My name—the year—the day.
As onward from the spot I passed,

5

One lingering look behind I cast—
A wave came rolling, high and fast,
    And washed my lines away.

And so, methought, 'twill shortly be
With every mark on earth from me ;
A wave of dark oblivion's sea
    Will sweep across the place
Where I have trod the sandy shore
Of time,—and been, to be no more ;—
Of me, my name, the name I bore,
    To leave no track nor trace.

And yet, with Him who counts the sands
And holds the waters in His hands,
I know a lasting record stands
    Inscribed against my name,
Of all this mortal part has wrought,
Of all this thinking soul has thought,—
And from these fleeting moments caught—
    For glory or for shame.

ANNE GARDNER HALE.

Miss Hale was born in Newburyport, Mass., August
5, 1823, and was daughter of Jacob and Mary Jane
(Hoyt) Hale. She was educated at Miss Sarah Ann
Wade's private school for young ladies, and at Roger
S. Howard's select school, in her native city. She began to rhyme when a child, and to write verses at the
age of thirteen, first appearing in print at the age of sev-

enteen. She at first published her effusions anonymously, subsequently signing her initials, an asterisk, or
a letter of the alphabet taken at random, and sometimes
two or more letters taken consecutively. She, also, sometimes wrote over the name of "Alice Hawthorne," and
of "Edith May," using the latter name until she learned
that there was another " Edith May." She at length
signed her own full name. Her efforts have been published in more than twenty different publications. Her
prose writings consist of two volumes of stories, a pamphlet, book reviews, essays, and papers on various top-
ics. She is a ready writer, and her utterances are fine,
true, and high-minded. Her style is sometimes quaint,
and she is often witty and weird. She is about prepar-
ing a volume of her poems for the press. She has a san-
guine-nervous temperament, and a passion for books,
music, and wild-flowers. Her home is one of those
old-fashioned, square three-story houses, with wide halls
and large, high rooms, which are characteristic of the
quaint old city of Newburyport, where she has always
resided. From her windows she can look down upon
the dreamy vistas of morning light stretching out over
the harbor bar and sand dunes, and watch the sea in
all its varied moods.

GRASS.

The stately oak and the graceful vine,
    And flowers that brighten vale and hill,
Will live in the poet's flowing line
    So long as his measures the heart-strings thrill ;—

I strike my lyre to a humbler theme—
   Yet worthier far of the world's proud lays—
So long neglected, the task I deem
   My own to yield it its claim of praise.

I sing the grass, the homely grass,
   That bows at the breath of the passing wind.
Its gifts in value to man surpass
   Rich ore of Ophir and gems of Ind ;
And the eye that sees in the dew-drop's sheen
   The beauty that glows in the rainbow's arch
Can trace in the meadow's garb of green
   Of its upward glory the wondrous march.

Despised—down-trodden—it springs aloft,
   On the ladder of earthly needs up-sent,
From the sleek kine grazing around the croft
   To the soul's strength gathered from pure health lent.
For ever the noblest of earth depends
   On this humblest link in the chain of power,
And the vigorous frame to the soul extends
   Its faithful services hour on hour.

So I sing the praise of the waving grass,
   Along the road, or on fertile lea ;
Whose serried armies of blades surpass
   The hosts overwhelmed in war's red sea ;
Who peacefully battle from age to age
   Against gaunt famine and his allies,—
No nobler theme can the muse engage
   Than these conquerors' deeds of high emprise !

O, the grass so green in the springtime gay,
  Or its golden plenty of perfect grain,
Or its fragrant breath in the new-mown hay,
  Shall ever my grateful praises gain !
To the homely grass that lays at our feet,
  In its deep humility, blessings high !
Nor kings of the forest, nor blossoms sweet,
  Shall hide its worth from the earnest eye.

LOUISA JANE HALL.

MRS. HALL was born in Newburyport, Mass., February 2, 1802, and was daughter of Dr. John and Louisa
(Adams) Park. The family removed to Boston when
she was about two years old, and in 1811 her father
opened a school for young ladies, partly that she might
have the best advantages in obtaining an education and
at the same time be under his immediate care. She
was an industrious scholar, and the thoroughness of her
study shows itself all through her works by her chaste and
correct style. She continued in her father's school until she was seventeen. At the age of twenty, she began
to publish poems, anonymously, in the *Literary Gazette*, and other papers and magazines. She lacked con-
fidence in her own powers, and was always distrustful
of the public reception of her articles. She would have
written much more but for this reason, together with ill-
health and impaired eye-sight. She also published a
historical tale, and a biography of Elizabeth Carter, the

English authoress. Allibone says that few American poetical compositions have been more highly commended than "Miriam," a drama in verse, Mrs. Hall's finest work, which was written in 1826. In 1831, the family removed to Worcester, and in 1840 she married Rev. Edward B. Hall, a Unitarian minister of Providence, R. I., where they afterward lived. Mr. Hall died in 1866, and his widow continued to reside in Providence until 1872, when she removed to Boston, where she has since resided. She is the oldest of the Essex county poets that are still alive.

A volume of Mrs. Hall's writings, entitled "Verse and Prose," was published in 1850.

———

EXTRACT FROM "MIRIAM."

Thraseno. Where wouldst thou seek for peace or
　　quietness,
If not beside the altar of thy God?
Miriam. Within these mighty walls of sceptred
　　Rome
A thousand temples rise unto her gods,
Bearing their lofty domes unto the skies,
Graced with the proudest pomp of earth ; their shrines
Glittering with gems, their stately colonnades,
Their dreams of genius wrought into bright forms,
Instinct with grace and godlike majesty,
Their ever-smoking altars, white-robed priests,
And all the pride of gorgeous sacrifice.

And yet these things are naught.   Rome's prayers as-
    cend
To greet th' unconscious skies, in the blue void
Lost like the floating breath of frankincense,
And find no hearing or acceptance there.
And yet there *is* an Eye that ever marks
Where its own people pay their simple vows,
Though to the rocks, the caves, the wilderness,
Scourged by a stern and ever-watchful foe !
There *is* an Ear that hears the voice of prayer
Rising from lonely spots where Christians meet,
Although it stir not more the sleeping air
Than the soft waterfall, or forest breeze.
Thinks't thou, my father, this benignant God
Will close His ear, and turn in wrath away
From the poor sinful creature of His hand,
Who breathes in solitude her humble prayer?
Thinks't thou He will not hear me, should I kneel
Here in the dust beneath His starry sky,
And strive to raise my voiceless thoughts to Him,
Making an altar of my broken heart?

ALICE CORA HAMMOND.

Mrs. Hammond was born in January, 1851, in Texas,
at "Deeron's Point," near Matagorda, the peninsula having since been entirely washed away in a very severe
storm. She was the daughter of William Farrington and

Alice Williams (Bridges) Oliver, both of whom were Northern people. When she was about four years of age, a tornado swept away their property and very nearly themselves. This decided her father to return to the North. Soon after doing so, he concluded to settle in Lynn, Mass., where his relatives resided and where he was born. There the family have since lived. Alice studied in the public schools, and afterward taught in them three years, at the end of which time she married Mr. Charles A. Hammond of that city, superintendent of the Boston and Revere Beach Railroad. She began to write when quite young, and her early effusions were published in the local papers. She has since contributed poems to *The Christian Union, New York Home Journal, Portland Transcript, New York Observer, The Watchman, Golden Days, The Californian Magazine, The Chicago Ledger,* and *Cottage Hearth.* One of her youthful poems, entitled "Only," has been set to music by "Virginia Gabriel" in this country, and also by an English composer. For the last two or three years she has done but little literary work on account of her numerous family cares.

THE LITTLE " CHORISTER. "

In the early summer morning, while the dew gleams on
    the grass,
And the flying, fleecy cloudlets make strange shadows
    as they pass,

Through the wide, old-fashioned doorway comes the
    tread of marching feet,
And a tuneless, timeless singing in a baby's accent sweet.
Soon the chanting voice comes nearer, and within the
    doorway stands
Smallest " chorister" that ever held a note-book in his
    hands ;
Curly head full proudly lifted, blue eyes fastened on his
    "score"
(Sure a sober daily paper never met such use before).
Smiling lips send forth the "music"— shade of Mozart !
    what a strain !
While the small, uncertain footsteps strive to keep the
    "time," in vain.
Not in minster or cathedral e'er were heard such strains
    of yore ;
And I listen till the chanting dies away without the
    door.
Ah, my baby, if, outgrowing all thy childhood's words
    and ways,
Thou shalt keep thy joyous spirit that seems ever giv-
    ing praise,
Or if in the choir of angels thou shalt sing *Te Deums*
    grand,
No one knoweth save our Father ; all thy times are in
    His hand ;
Yet on memory's page emblazoned shall I see thee,
    passing fair,
Smiling, singing, with the sunshine trembling in thy
    golden hair.

PHEBE ANNE HANAFORD.

Mrs. Hanaford was born on the Island of Nantucket, Mass., May 6, 1829, and was daughter of George Washington and Phebe Ann (Barnard) Coffin, both of whom were Quakers. She studied in the schools of her native place until she was fifteen, and afterward continued her studies with her rector. She began to write in rhyme when very young, her earliest remembered verses having been written when eight years old. Her poems first appeared in print when she was thirteen. She was married in 1849, taught school a year at Newton, then resided in her native place till 1857, at which time, with her family, she removed to Beverly, and became active in the temperance cause. In 1864, she removed to Reading, and from 1866 for three years she was editor of the *Ladies' Repository* and *The Myrtle*. In 1866 she commenced preaching in Hingham, and in 1868 was ordained pastor of the First Universalist church there, being the first woman ever ordained to the gospel ministry in New England. During the year 1869, she preached at both Hingham and Waltham, then in New Haven, Conn., for four years, subsequently in Jersey City, N. J., until 1884, when she returned to New Haven, where with voice and pen she is still actively engaged in the Master's service. In 1870, she served several times as chaplain in the Connecticut legislature, and also in 1872, being the first woman ever called to act in that capacity. She has published twelve volumes of prose, some of them having had immense sales. She is a favorite lecturer, a successful preacher, and a worker for woman suffrage, and all reforms of the times.

Mrs. Hanaford's largest collection of poems is entitled "From Shore to Shore, and Other Poems," and was published, with her portrait, in 1871.

MOONLIGHT ON THE OCEAN.

'Tis moonlight on the ocean; and the mighty waters
    sleep,
Save where the line of radiance comes across the path-
    less deep :
There billows weave a fairy dance, and sparkle in the
    light
Which falls so softly on them now, amid the hush of
    night.

I stand upon the hilltop green, and gaze far o'er the
    main,
And see the rocky islets there, and hear the waves
    again,
Which beat in gentle cadences upon the pebbly shore,
And whisper of a distant isle my eyes may see no more.

Home, home, beyond those waters ! O home so dear to
    me !
Not e'en the crested billows can divide my heart from
    thee.

Are moonbeams resting on the waves which break along
    thy shore ?
And do the eyes I long to greet gaze on them as before ?

Moonlight upon the ocean : oh ! there is no fairer scene
This side the pearly gates of heaven, for mortal eyes, I
    ween ;
And, while I gaze, my heart ascends with grateful praise
    to Him
Before whose bounteous holiness the sheen of earth
    grows dim.

Father and Savior ! Spirit pure ! my heart ascends to
    thee,
That, wheresoe'er upon this earth my weary feet may be,
My eyes may gaze on scenes so fair through faith's re-
    vealing glass,
That trustfully toward future days my steps may onward
    pass.

For He who sends the moonlight now to make the deep
    so fair—
God's smile upon the waters dark when gloomy night
    is there—
Can send his spirit's joyful light to gleam along my
    way,—
A line of holy radiance and a part of heaven's day.

O God ! I thank thee for the hours, when standing by
    the sea,
Alone, or with beloved friends, my heart is drawn to
    thee ;

For, while its quiet loveliness my spirit doth control,
This moonlight on the ocean shall be sunlight in my
soul.

—*Beverly, Sept. 30, 1859.*

HIRAM BETTS HASKELL.

MR. HASKELL was born in Frederickton, New Brunswick, January 17, 1823, and was son of Caleb and
Fanny Matilda (Betts) Haskell. When he was about
five years of age, the family removed to Newburyport,
Mass., where he was reared, being educated in the common schools. He was for a while a clerk in a grocery
store, and then went to Boston, where he pursued the
drug business until he was about twenty-three years old.
He devoted the remainder of his life to portrait painting,
for which he possessed considerable talent and skill. He
was also a lecturer, an actor and an editor. He wrote
for the *Newburyport Daily Union,* and other papers, in
both prose and verse, his poetry always being good, and
many of his efforts fine. He was never married, and
spent most of his life in his bachelor quarters in Newburyport. He was extremely sensitive and tender in
his nature, having a strong sense of truth and honor,
and being generous to a fault, with not a particle of love
for money or money-getting. He was agreeable and
entertaining in society ; but when at work his attention
was entirely absorbed in what he was doing. While
painting a portrait at Byfield parish, Newbury, he was

found in his room there one morning, in an unconscious
state, and thus remained till his death, which occurred
two days later, August 22, 1873, at the age of fifty.

"The half finished portrait on the easel,
  The pencil and the palette lying still,
    With no more rhythm from the point of quill;
  His work was done, whether ill or well."

TRUTH AND BEAUTY.

Truth welleth up by beauty's side :
Whoe'er shall seek its crystal tide
Shall see the gems that flash below,
The flowers that on its borders grow,—
Yet fearful is the timid world
    Amid romantic haunts to stray,
Where beauty's banner is unfurled,
    Lest it should meet upon its way
    Some syren singing to betray.

Be faithful, brothers, and believe ;
The beautiful can ne'er deceive.
Look up into the tranquil sky,
And see if thou canst read a lie ;
All pictured o'er with glorious clouds,
Like kings in bridal robes and shrouds,
Or eloquent with starry light
Seeking to cheer the sad, sweet night.

Look on the field and forest green,
On sunny hill and dark ravine ;

Still looking till thy gaze hath met
The windings of the rivulet;
Where'er the reverend eye may roam
This knowledge to thy mind will come :
Infinite wisdom, power and love
Is written on the heavens above,
And on the grassy, flowery sod,
Each quivering leaf is lisping God;
That beauty is but truth unbound,
And clad in colors and encrowned;
Truth, bursting into bud and bloom,
    Truth, rounding into form and grace,
The breaking of the light through gloom,
    To gladden all the lonely space ;
For He, who made the ocean, gave
The foam-crest to the marching wave ;
Who flung the myriad orbs on high,
Gave all its beauty to the sky.

The beautiful is always true,
    And falsehood hath no symmetry,—
Falling upon my heart like dew,
    With soothing power this comes to me.
Are not the oracles of song
    True as the dull logician's proof?
Where science throws her warp along
    Beauty flies through the flowery woof.
There is not in the poet's dream,
Or in the bold reformer's scheme,
One thought baptized by beauty's kiss

But brings at last its promised bliss ;
Whether in carol, code, or creed,
'Twill work its symbol in some deed.

May aught in human bosom prove
More loving than almighty love ?
Aught fairer in the poet's mind
Than the Great Artist hath designed?
No !—in the wildest glens of thought,
    Where'er the flowers of fancy grow,
Each little bud, each leaf, hath caught
A spark from Heaven's eternal glow.

———

LUCY HOOPER.

Miss Hooper was born in Newburyport, Mass., February 4, 1816, and was daughter of Joseph and Mary
(Whittemore) Hooper.   From her father, who was a
merchant and a man of decided piety, strong mind and
cultivation, Lucy received her general education.   As a
child she was docile, and full of quiet affection and rev-
erence.   She had a strong desire to extend her studies,
but her delicate health forbade.   She was passionately
fond of chemistry, ancient and modern history, literature,
the languages, and natural history, especially botany.
When she was fifteen years old, the family removed to
Brooklyn, N. Y., where she afterward resided until her
death.   As soon as she was settled in her new home she
began to contribute to *The Long Island Star*, and other

periodicals, over her initials only. She wrote prose, also, but loved best to express her thoughts and feelings in verse, which seemed so natural to her. The loss of her father and many other relatives and friends by death, and her own slow but sure malady, consumption, saddened all her thoughts, and shed a melancholy over her efforts. A few weeks before her death she prepared a work, entitled "The Lady's Book of Flowers and Poetry," which was published in 1845. She wrote with taste, reflection and good judgment. This sweet, gifted, and pure girl died at Brooklyn August 1, 1841, at the age of twenty-five.

In 1842, "The Literary Remains of Miss Hooper," with a memoir by the eloquent John Keese, was published; and in 1848, her "Complete Poetical Works" was issued.

———

"*IT IS WELL.*"

'Twas a low grave they led me to, o'ergrown
With violets of the spring, and starry moss,
And all the sweet wild flowerets that disclose
Their hues and fragrance round the dreamless couch,
As if to tell how quietly the head
That here had throbbed so feverishly, doth rest.
'Twas a low grave, and the soft zephyrs played
Gently around it; and the setting sun
Gleamed brightly on the marble at its head,
Bearing the date—the name—the few brief years,
Of one whose blessed lot it was to pass

6

To the fair land of promise, ere the chill
And blight of this dark world had power to cast
A shade on life's pure blossom ; while the dew
Of morning was upon its leaves, and all
The outward world was beauty ; ere the eye
Had ever wept in secret, or the heart
Grown heavy with a sorrow unconfessed.
Was it a bitter lot?   That stainless stone
Answered the query ; but one line it bore—
One brief inscription, thrilling the deep heart
Of those who, leaning o'er that narrow mound,
Mused over life's vain sorrow :
                              " It is well."
Ay, the deep words had meaning ; but what grief
Had taught the lone survivors thus to count
The sum of all, and, struggling with their tears,
Write only—"It is well"? Oh ! well for her
To rest on that green earth—to lay the head
Unwearied on its bosom, and to seek
A refuge from the coldness of the world,
Ere yet its shaft had pierced her.
                              "It is well."
And, oh ! for us who, musing o'er that grave,
Sigh for the rest a stranger's breast hath found,
Were it not well, in the heart's hour of grief,
When earth is dim, and all her shining streams
Discourse no more in music to our ears—
When shadows rest upon her brightest flowers,
And the continued sorrow of the soul
Doth darken sun and moon, to dream at last

Of a still rest beneath the lowly stone—
A calm, unbroken slumber, where the eye
Shall weep no more in sadness, and the pulse
Forget its quick, wild throbbings?
                O'er that grave
Such were my musings, till a deeper truth
Broke on my mind, as the blue violet shed
Its sweetness round me, and the evening winds
Brought fragrance from afar ; and then I prayed,
In lowliness of heart, that I might bear
In faith "The heat and burden of the day,"
And never, till His purpose was fulfilled,
And every errand He had set performed
In trusting patience, sigh for dreamless rest,
Nor till th' impartial pen of truth could write
Above that quiet refuge— "It is well."

LOUISA PARSONS HOPKINS.

Mrs. Hopkins was born in Newburyport, Mass.,
April 19, 1834, and was daughter of Jacob and Eliza
(Atkins) Stone, both of them being people of marked
character. At the age of sixteen she graduated from the
Putnam Free School in her native town, and afterward
from the State Normal School. She then assumed the
profession of a teacher, and after a few years of successful endeavor in that capacity she married Mr. John
Hopkins, a gentleman of New Bedford, becoming the
mother of a large family. She has always been a labo-

rious student. She is widely interested in educational affairs, connected with which she has published a number of volumes, and is at present one of the supervisors of the Boston schools. In 1881, she printed her first volume of poems, entitled " Motherhood, " which aroused the warmest admiration, some of the strains being pronounced Miltonic. This was followed by "Persephone," a remarkable and subtle poem, full of beauty and music, and insight into the depths of nature. Mrs. Hopkins is very attractive in her appearance ; she is grey-eyed, her hair is nearly blonde in color, and the features of her face are cut with the precision of a cameo. She is an entertaining companion, and her highly wrought religious temperament has never interfered with a great love of fun, nor her enthusiasms with her keen penetration. A few years ago she returned to her native place, where she has a beautiful home on the banks of the Merrimac.

———

NONQUITT.

.Summer has flashed her golden shuttle by
    My dreaming eye,
Her shining web of days, so soft and fair,
    Without a care
Is folding down into the silent past
    Too bright to last.

Night unto night has told its peace serene
    While Luna, queen,

Paved her white shimmering path above the deep,
That stirred in sleep
To lisp its dreamy bliss around the shore
Forevermore.

Day unto day ushered its beauty in
With happy din,
Thrush and song-sparrow trilling through the hours,
While myriad flowers
Bespangled dewy grass and fragrant wood,
And all was good.

The odorous breeze wafted its music round,—
A varied sound.
Called from the wide campaign the whistling quail,
The tern's shrill wail
Answered afar, and boomed from rock to rock
The billow's shock.

Here have I sat without my cottage door
And watched the shore,
Followed its curving line to where the town
Lies sloping down,
Its clustering gems in simple beauty set,—
Fair coronet !

And still along its amber thread of strand
Stretches the land,
Till the grim fortress at the harbour's mouth
Looks threatening, south,
But hears no sound save dash of sprays that wet
Its parapet.

Then on and on the rippling waters spread
    By cliff and head,
By long low neck, and sunny sanded isles,
    The blue bay smiles,
Till like a soul within the conscious seas
    Sits Penikese.

And to and fro the opal sails have sped,
    Or glimmered red
The seven coast-lights about the land-locked bay,
    While night and day
The broad blue sky with sun or star has lit
    Light-bathed Nonquitt.

But now the slopes are shadowing with wings,
    And southward swings
The clamoring host of swallows o'er the sea ;
    'Tis time for me
To seek my closer eaves, and, sighing, fold
    This cloth of gold.

MARY LAMBERT HORTON.

MISS HORTON was born in that part of Danvers, Mass., which is now Peabody, February 15, 1805, and was daughter of Lemuel and Hannah (Porter) Horton. Her mind matured at a very early age, and she was uncommonly interesting. Her early life was the dawning of a genius, which, under proper cultivation, would in after years have shone with brilliancy, and attained a high position in the world of letters. An extended education was the object of her constant and eager desire, but her physical weakness would not allow the necessary application. In spite of her hindrances and discouragements, she improved her talents, and spoke and wrote with readiness and excellence. She began her literary work at a very early period, founding most of her articles upon every-day events. She had an ardent affection for the truth, a rich imagination, and a justness of observation. She had a deep poetic nature ; pensiveness being the peculiar characteristic of her productions. She wrote for the *Marblehead Register* and *Salem Register*, over the *nom de plume* of "M. Louisa," and also over her three initials. She possessed a lovely character, and was the ornament and solace of her mother's home, gladdening and supporting her daily steps. After a long sickness, with consumption, she died, in a blissful state of mind, in Salem, on Sunday, August 28, 1831, at the age of twenty-six.

The next year after Miss Horton's decease, her "Poetical and Prose Compositions" were published in a very small and thin bound volume.

———

MOONLIGHT REVERIES.

Silent and beautiful ! I've watched thee, till
Imagination soared beyond the far
Blue curtains of thy palace ; and I've wished—
How ardently I've wished, to turn aside
The azure covering of the star-lit world,

And learn its secret ! send my gaze
Beyond the blue exterior, and convey
Back to inquiring earth, eternity's soft answer.

But most of all,
To hold communion with celestial souls,
Who once were mortal ! dear departed ones
Who loved, instructed, cheered, and cherished us
Through life's trod valleys.

O could I learn
The nature, image, wishes, and the thoughts
Of parted spirits ! whether death
Has closed the mortal sympathies, and stayed
The life-tide of affection—severed all
The tender ties of nature, and congealed
The fountain of remembrance—or strung
The sympathies anew, and let more free
Affection's life-tide ; more firm united
Nature's every tie, and waked
New strains to memory.

EDWARD GILBERT HULL.

MR. HULL was born June 1, 1834, in Bradford, Mass.,
in that portion of the town which has since been incor-
porated as the town of Groveland, and was son of Darius and Sarah Fowler (Hardy) Hull. Living at home
during his minority he attended the district school and
acquired considerable education. When the war of the
Rebellion broke out, he volunteered to defend the Un-

ion cause, and served at the front as a sergeant in the Twenty-third Regiment of the Massachusetts troops, accompanying it with General Burnside in the expedition to Newbern and Roanoke Island. At the termination of his service he returned to his native hills, and a few years later removed to the neighboring town of Ipswich, which he made his residence. There he soon became an office-holder, constituting one of the board of selectmen of that ancient town for several years. Being esteemed by the people he was chosen to represent the district, of which Ipswich then constituted a part, in the Massachusetts House of Representatives for 1879. He has since that time given a considerable portion of his time to literary pursuits, having, besides his prose compositions, written some five hundred poems, very many of which have been published. He is possessed of talent as a poet, and has written some pretty songs and occasional pieces. He still resides in Ipswich, and at the present time is engaged on the *Independent*, one of the Ipswich newspapers, being one of the editors.

In 1886, Mr. Hull published "A Collection of Miscellaneous Poems, with Drama," a bound volume of duodecimo size.

ERIN.

Far away in Emerald Erin, as the poets term the land,
Where the roses bloom more sweetly and the breezes are more bland ;

Where the skies are ever beaming with a deeper, tenderer blue ;
Where the winding rivers wander on through vales of
greener hue ;

In a peasant's humble cottage, by the Shannon's rolling
tide ;
All as free from art's devices as its inmates are from
pride ;
In that low and humble cottage, plain and simple
though it be,
I have left my heart behind me far away beyond the
sea.

For the fairest flower that ever decked the vales of
Erin's Isle,
Patient there awaits my coming with a fond and trust-
ing smile ;
Wanders out at noon and even to the sacred trysting
tree,
Sending forth her sweetest blessings o'er the rolling tide
to me.

What were all the wealth I'm seeking, all the treasures
that I gain ?
All life's golden days before me, all the hopes I enter-
tain ?
All these blissful dreams of pleasure, all I strive or wish
to be,
Were it not for that sweet maiden far away beyond the
sea.

Fast the fleeting tide rolls onward to the dear appointed
    day,
When the filling sails will waft me to my native land
    away;
When the bounding bark shall bear me to my waiting
    Nora's side,
To the cottage in the valley by the Shannon's rolling
    tide.

Though Columbia's shores are ringing with her free-
    men's happy tones,
Though her hills and vales are dotted with a million
    happy homes;
I'll go back to sunny Erin, thrice fair but yet less free,
For I've left my heart behind me, far away beyond the
    sea.

ANNIE ELIZA JOHNSON.

MRS. JOHNSON was born in Nahant, Mass., August
19, 1827, and was daughter of Jonathan and Anna
(Stone) Johnson. She studied in the public school of
her native place, and subsequently attended Mrs. Putnam's private school in Reading, and the Lynn Academy. In 1849, she had the great sorrow of losing, by
death, her only sister, a loss which clouded her life ever
after, and which, perhaps, has influenced considerably
all that she has since written. The next year, she became the wife of her second cousin, Mr. Charles Benjamin Johnson of Lynn, and has two children, a son and

a daughter. After her marriage, she continued to reside in Nahant, which is still her home. In winter, this
popular summer resort is a very quiet and isolated place,
yet having always lived here, she has become so accus-
tomed to its seclusion that she does not wish for any
other home. Outside of literary work, hers has been
the life of the greater portion of wives and mothers, ever
doing her many duties in a quiet, unostentatious way.
She has only written verses, and contributed them to
the *Boston Atlas, Boston Traveller, Rambler, New
England Farmer, Christian Register, Daily Evening
Transcript, New York Christian Leader, Salem Register, Lynn News, Lynn Reporter, Lynn Transcript,* and
other papers, and for the *Ladies' Repository,* and other
magazines. Her poetry has the genius and sweetness
of a Moore, and ranks among the best productions of
our poets.

———

THE BELLS OF LYNN.

Far, far and wide, across the sea—
  Farther than wild winds ever flung
The cadence of their melody—
  A poet hath their praises sung.

In pleasant lands across the sea,
  The magic of his song doth win
From kindly hearts, in pleasant homes,
  Sweet praises for the bells of Lynn.

To me how many thoughts they bring
  Of childhood's day, its smiles and tears,—
Ah, never more such chimes may ring
  As gladdened all those happy years !

We hear the cheerful bells at noon ;
  And closing the brief winter-day ;
We, listening, wait, when "nine" at night
  Rings, clear and sweet, across the bay.

But sweeter still, o'er summer seas,
  Their distant music sinks and swells,
Now lost 'mid ocean-symphonies,
  Now like a peal of fairy bells.

I see the gleaming lights shine out
  Across the bay. Above the din
Of stormy winds and waves, how clear
  Ring out, to-night, the bells of Lynn !

SAMUEL JOHNSON.

MR. JOHNSON was born in Salem, Mass., October 10, 1822, and was son of Dr. Samuel and Anna (Dodge) Johnson. His boyhood was promising, and was passed under influences favorable to its fullest development. He was prepared for college in private schools in his native place, and graduated at Harvard University in 1842. He entered the Cambridge divinity school, from which he graduated in 1846. He became a Unitarian minister, and, without ordination, preached in Boston for one year.   His anti-slavery sentiments gave offence, and he left Boston in 1853, going to Lynn, where he was pastor of a free church until 1870. His advanced views were not in accordance with the ideas of the Unitarian denomination generally, and he retired to the ancestral home in North Andover, where he spent the remainder of his life in study and authorship. He died there February 19, 1882, at the age of fifty-nine years.   In disposition he was pleasant, especially in his family, where his exuberant gladness flowed full and free.   He was tender and faithful, with zeal for justice, freedom and truth.   He worshiped the great truths underlying all forms and creeds, though never a materialist.   He is said to have been an enemy to Christianity, but he sought nothing more nor less than the worship of the Creator in spirit and in truth.   He was an able poet, and the author of "Oriental Religions."   He was also eloquent as an orator, being possessed of rare talent and culture.

With Rev. Samuel Longfellow, Mr. Johnson published " Hymns of the Spirit " in 1846.

A memorial of Mr. Johnson, with his photograph, was published in 1882.

INSPIRATION.

Life of ages, richly poured,
　Love of God, unspent and free,
Flowing in the prophet's word
　And the people's liberty !

Never was to chosen race
That unstinted tide confined ;
Thine in every time and place,
Fountain sweet of heart and mind !

Secret of the morning stars,
Motion of the oldest hours,
Pledge through elemental wars
Of the coming spirit's powers !

Rolling planet, flaming sun,
Stand in nobler man complete ;
Prescient laws thine errands run,
Frame the shrine for Godhead meet.

Homeward led, the wondering eye
Upward yearned in joy or awe,
Found the love that waited nigh,
Guidance of thy guardian law.

In the touch of earth it thrilled ;
Down from mystic skies it burned ;
Right obeyed and passion stilled
Its eternal gladness earned.

Breathing in the thinker's creed,
Pulsing in the hero's blood,
Nerving simplest thought and deed,
Freshening time with truth and good,

Consecrating art and song,
Holy book and pilgrim track,

Hurling floods of tyrant wrong
From the sacred limits back,—

Life of ages, richly poured,
Love of God, unspent and free,
Flow still in the prophet's word
And the people's liberty !

HENRY COGSWELL KNIGHT.

MR. KNIGHT was born in Hampton, N. H., in 1788, and was the son of Joseph and Elizabeth (Cogswell) Knight. When Harry was very young he lost his mother, and in his boyhood his father also died. He then went to reside with his maternal grandfather, Dr. Cogswell, in Rowley, Mass. Here he had a home which was delightful to his nature. The house stood in the midst of trees, always luxuriant, and alive with birds, whose songs made life very pleasant. He found here intellectual and polished society, and the simple and rural life for which he longed. He attended Dummer Academy, and graduated at Brown University in 1812. He studied theology, and May 6, 1827, was ordained a deacon of the Protestant Episcopal Church, by the bishop of Massachusetts. He was afterward ordained to the priesthood, and became a rector, serving in several parishes. As a writer, and especially as a poet, he became well-known. He had a want of decision, and always felt as if he had made a mistake in the choice of his profession. So in his literary work, he lacked that con-

fidence in himself which success demands. He resided
in Boston two or three years, and returned to Rowley
a year or two before his death, which occurred there
January 10, 1835, at the age of forty-six.

Beside "Letters from the South and West," over the
signature of "Arthur Singleton," printed in 1824, and
two volumes entitled "Lectures and Sermons," in 1831,
Mr. Knight published several volumes of poems, as follows: "The Cypriad," in 1809; "The Trophies of
Love;" "The Broken Harp," in 1815; and "Poems,"
in two volumes, in 1821.

———

THE LITTLE SWEEP.

Sweep chimney, sweep !
Sweep chimney, sweep !
    Pity the boy
    Without employ,
The snow is very deep ;
    O pity take,
    For misery's sake,
Nor leave him cold to weep—
Poor little Afric sweep !

He's very cold ;
Oh ! very cold ;
    With nought to eat,
    And frozen feet,
His doublet now grown old ;
    His shoes are torn,

This snowy morn,
And oh ! was Sampo sold
To die with winter's cold ?

None hear my cry ;
Soon I must die ;
For in the street,
No one I meet,
While in the snow I cry ;
Ah ! now I know,
In sheets of snow,
Poor Sampo cold must lie—
Ah ! with his brush must die.

LUCY LARCOM.

Miss Larcom was born at the "Farms" in Beverly,
Mass., March 5, 1824, and was daughter of Benjamin
and Lois (Barrett) Larcom.   The first ten years of her
life were passed in her native town, to which she has
always been filially attached.   Her second decade was
spent at Lowell, where for a time she was employed as
an operative in the mills, and where she began to write,
her earliest articles, both prose and verse, appearing in
The Lowell Offering, to which she continued to be a
favorite contributor.   She afterward went to Illinois,
where she taught and studied, graduating at Monticello
Seminary, in that state, after a three years' course of instruction.   In 1852, she returned to Massachusetts and
taught a young-ladies' school in Beverly, subsequently

teaching for six years in the Wheaton Seminary, at Norton. Since then she has taught in several academies and seminaries. She still occasionally teaches or lectures in young-ladies' schools, and resides at Beverly Farms. While the magazine, entitled *Our Young Folks*, was in existence, she was its leading editor for a year or two. She has written almost all of her life, having contributed to *The Lowell Courier, Sartain's Union Magazine, The Crayon*, and other periodicals. Her poetry, much of which relates to Beverly and its vicinity, is of a pleasant sort, and will long find a welcome in every household. Her genius is particularly happy in putting into verse the events of every-day life.

Miss Larcom has published several volumes of poems ; her "Poems" in 1869 ; "An Idyl of Work" in 1874 ; "Wild Roses of Cape Ann ;" and "Poetical Works," with portrait, in 1884.

IN THE RAIN.

A light flashed up in her sad blue eye,
Like a ray through a break in the cloudy sky,
    As she leaned at the showered pane.
"Thank Heaven ! he's come !"—but the train shrieked
    "Nay !"
And crashed o'er her dying hopes away.
    Still she waited on
    Till the day was gone,
  Waited alone in the rain.

Ever, now and again, the cloud-rack through
There peeped a bud of the heavenly blue,—
  Blue without speck or stain.
Then the young corn shook in its jewelled mist,
And the violets twinkled, pure amethyst ;
   And her eye grew bright
   With a dewy light,
  Waiting alone in the rain.

But the soft blue flower of the sky shut up
Behind the tempest its hollow cup ;
  The meadows were dim again :
And the warm light faded out of her eyes,
While she paced, and gazed on the restless skies,
   While she tried to keep
   Her wild heart asleep,
  Waiting alone in the rain.

It streamed and poured from the shelving bank ;
It sprinkled mire on the sedges rank ;
  It beat on the springing grain.
"Come home !" called the horn from behind the hill :
She heard, but she lingered and listened still,
   Still, gazing back
   Down the iron track,
  Waited alone in the rain.

The hours dragged by ; it was dark and late ;
The cars rushed on with their throbbing freight,
  Screaming a laugh at her pain.
But the west uncurtained a wide, clear space,

And the sunset lighted a laggard face,
And the wild, wet day
Stole in smiles away,
While two hurried home in the rain.

ALONZO LEWIS.

ALONZO LEWIS, only son of Zachariah and Mary
(Hudson) Lewis, was born in Lynn, Mass., August 28,
1794. He received a thorough education, and became
proficient in many languages. He delighted to teach,
and was at one time head master of the Lynn Academy.
In 1831 he established a school for young ladies in Boston, and taught until 1835. He wrote and published
a history of Lynn, an English grammar and a work on
geometry. During his whole life he wrote both prose
and poetry for current periodicals, and edited an anti-
slavery paper in Lynn before Mr. Garrison began to
publish the *Liberator*, of which paper, and also of the
Boston Traveller, he was for a time editorially in charge.
He had a religious and benevolent nature, and led a
consistent Christian life, attending services at St. Peter's
church in Salem, to which he walked every Sunday until the Episcopal church in Lynn was established. His
poetic talent displayed itself quite early in life, some of
his poems having been written at the age of seventeen.
He wrote much and well; the efforts of his younger
years being thought the best. The latter portion of his
life he spent with his family in his picturesque cottage

in his native town close to the edge of the water, by which he delighted to sit and ponder and study. Here, the "Bard of Lynn," as he was early called, died January 21, 1861, at the age of sixty-six.

In 1823 Mr. Lewis' poems were first published in a volume; and in 1831 and 1834 appeared other volumes. They went through fourteen editions. The last one, which was edited by his son Ion Lewis, with portrait and biographical sketch, was published in 1883.

STANZAS.

I made me a little bark,
And trusted my all on board;
And her sails were spread like the wings of the lark,
Though the storm was on, and the waves were dark,
And the winds and the waters roared.

But soon the sun looked from on high,
And stilled the stormy main;
And before his face the clouds did fly,
Leaving behind a clear blue sky,
And the ocean smiled again.

And still my bark went o'er the seas,
With a soft and rippling tune,
Like the gentle boughs of the forest trees,
That meet and kiss when stirred by the breeze,
In the leafy month of June.

And on she went with a motion as free
As the soaring, still-winged dove,
And stooped her side to the wave as meek
As the virgin bride, when she leans her cheek
To the first warm kiss of love.

But the sun went down and the night was dark,
And the stormy wind was high,
And the ocean waves went over the bark,
That saw neither land nor beacon-mark,
Nor the star-beam in the sky.

When lo ! a bright and cheering ray
Shone over the tide afar,
And I beheld, while my heart was gay
With the hope that rose on my erring way,
The bright and the morning star.

FANNIE SMILEY LOVEJOY.

MRS. LOVEJOY was born in Sidney, Maine, November
29, 1833, and was daughter of Asa and Sarah (Norton)
Smiley. Her parents were intellectual people, and members of the Society of Friends. She was an apt and dil-
igent scholar, and received her education in the common
schools and high school of her native place, and in private schools. In 1851 she married John Lovejoy of
West Newbury, Mass., where she has since resided.
She is now a widow, her husband having died a few
years ago. She began to compose poetry when quite

young, and first published her efforts at the age of sixteen. She has also written considerable prose. She has
contributed poems to the *Boston Transcript, Boston
Journal, Boston Home Journal, Our Little Ones,
Golden Days, Kennebec Journal, Gospel Banner,* and
local newspapers. She has the gift of poetry, and a
love for the grand and true and beautiful in nature and
humanity. She has an even temperament, and an overflow of mirthfulness, being possessed of good conversational powers. In prose she likes that which expresses
the strongest, deepest and most original thought, and in
poetry, that which comes from the divine nature within
us, and which is so inspiring and helpful, forever lifting
our thoughts above the earthly, and toward God.

FOR ALL.

The sun sends its bright rays of gladness
        Into the dreariest spot;
It lifts us from care and from sadness,
        It lightens the lowliest lot.
The stars shine out brightly above us
        When shadows of evening fall:
O, think how our Father must love us,—
        He gives his best unto all.

I climb the rough steeps of the mountain,
        And look, from its lofty brow,
On the verdure and rippling fountain
        And the bright flowers below;

I roam through the field and the forest,
    In nature's cool, shady hall
I list to the sweet, feathered chorist
    Warbling his tunes for us all.

I watch the grand waves of the ocean
    Rolling and lashing the shore,
Chanting in its ceaseless commotion
    The song of eternity's roar ;
And think its mysterious sounding,
    And music of brooklets' fall,
The beauty so rich and abounding,
    And grandeur sublime are for all.

The poor man is rich to inherit
    A love for these things in his mind,
The rich man is poor if his spirit
    To beauty and grandeur is blind ;
Come forth, child of care and of sadness,
    Nor linger where dark shadows fall,
Earth's greenness and sunshine and gladness
    And God's loving care are for all.

MARTHA PERRY LOWE.

Mrs. Martha Ann (Perry) Lowe was born in Keene, N. H., November 21, 1829, and was daughter of Justus and Hannah (Wood) Perry. Both of her parents died when she was thirteen years of age, and a few years later a brother and a sister died. Soon after these trials and sorrows, she went with her remaining

brother and sister to the West Indies, where they passed
the winter together.   Subsequently she went to Europe,
with her sister, and spent several months in Spain, where
her brother was serving as secretary of Legation.   She
passed the winter of 1856–7 in Salem, Mass., with her
sister, the wife of Dr. Edward B. Peirson, and while there
became acquainted with Rev. Charles Lowe, pastor of
the North Church in that city, whom she married the
following autumn.   Mr. Lowe had resigned his pastorate
in Salem two months prior to their marriage, but continued to reside there until 1859, when he was installed
over the Unitarian church in Somerville, whither they
removed.   He resigned this pastorate six years later
on account of his failing health, and was then editor of
the *Monthly Journal* from 1865 to 1869.   In 1871,
he went to Europe with his family, whence Mrs. Lowe
corresponded regularly for the *Liberal Christian.* They
returned home in 1873.   He died a few years since,
and she has published his biography.   She has since
resided in Somerville, being connected at the present
time with the *Unitarian Review.*   Her poems are much
admired.

Mrs. Lowe has published two volumes of poetry, one,
entitled "The Olive and the Pine," in 1859 ; and the
other, "Love in Spain, and Other Poems," in 1867.

THE ORGAN PLAYER.

He sat there at the great old organ's side
In mastery complete, and slowly laid

His fingers on the silent keys, and felt
Them o'er with groping hands, as he were rapt
Within the mazes of a wandering dream.

But, lo ! the waking ! Suddenly uprose
A mighty tempest of great notes, that rolled
Through all the carvéd space, and shook it from
Its boundless marble plains away unto
The spangled grayness of its lofty dome ;
And trembled in the arches, fading off
Till where they caught the rosy bloom that streamed
From little windows set with precious stones,
That looked aslant the vastness, cutting through
With rainbow mists the silent clouds of dark.
He is undaunted 'mid the whirlwind of
High ecstasy and pain, and joy and grief,
Which he hath wakened ; for his soul is far
Ascending to the upper dome that rests
Its beams not underneath the stars and sky,
Like this fair atom in the eye of heaven.
He sees his bride, who walketh in the light
That plays immortal in her hazel eyes,
And broods around her hair at rest in folds
Of placid brownness on her mellow cheek.

She is not roving 'mong the glorified,
Forgetful of the restless hearts on earth :
She watches him below with earnest eyes,
And lays her ear unto the floor of heaven
To catch the earthly sounds that wander up.

She follows close upon the organ's sweep
With voice of sweetness, full and deep and low—
He hears it,— 'mid the cooling shadow of
The great cathedral, hears it day and night,—
An undertone forever sounding clear
Throughout the torrent of his whelming chords.
Said he not, 'twere no mortal hands that ruled
The harmonies amid that solitude?
And so he sitteth there at morn and even,
And fondly dreameth that sometime he may
Float hence upon the current of her voice
Unto the high concerto of the skies !

CHARLES FLETCHER LUMMIS.

MR. LUMMIS was born in Lynn, Mass., March 1, 1859,
and was son of Prof. Henry and Harriet Waterman
(Fowler) Lummis. His mother died when he was but
two years old, and the family removed to and resided
in Tilton, N. H., for four years. He afterward lived in
Auburndale, and Lynn, Mass., until 1877, when he entered Harvard College. He lived in his native town
during his freshman year, when he became interested in
literature, and wrote a great number of verses for the
college press, and for the Boston, Lynn, St. Louis and
other papers. While in college he issued two tiny volumes, entitled "Birch-Bark Poems." They were printed
on birch-bark gathered at the White Mountains, and the
entire work was done by the author. The two volumes

have had an aggregate sale of over fourteen thousand copies. In 1882, he settled in Chillicothe, Ohio, the residence of his wife's parents, and became editor of the *Scioto Gazette*. While here he contributed regularly to *Life* and *The Judge*, and occasionally to *Puck*, *Texas Siftings*, *Detroit Free Press*, and other humorous papers, and to *Our Continent* and the *Atlantic Monthly*. In September, 1884, he started on a pedestrian tour across the continent. The trip took one hundred and forty-three days, in which he walked thirty-five hundred and seven miles. Feb. 1, 1885, he arrived at Los Angeles, Cal., where he has since resided. The story of his numerous adventures will appear in book form. In 1886, he was with General Crook, and later with General Miles in the campaign against Geronimo. Ever since settling in Los Angeles, he has been connected with the *Daily Times*, of which he is one of the editors and owners.

SUNSET ON PROFILE LAKE.

The westward sun has left a wake of flame
  Across the silent lake, upon whose breast
    The stern, still face, by wrathful tempests scarred,
Looks down impassive from the cliffs that frame
  The crystal waters as they lie at rest,
    Secure and trustful in his sleepless guard.

The regal trout, bestarred with gold and red,
  Shoots headlong high above his native tide
    In pure excess of joy, to greet the sun

Ere yet he seeks his far Pacific bed ;
And from the copses on the mountain-side
The rabbit leaps, a living streak of dun.

Upon the Old Man's brow one lingering ray
Still clings caressingly, as if God's hand
In radiant benediction rested there ;
And on the breezes' eddying currents, day
Drifts out beyond the dim horizon strand,
And night swims softly down the purple air.

GEORGE LUNT.

MR. LUNT was born in Newburyport, Mass., December 31, 1803, and was son of Abel and Phebe (Tilton) Lunt. He graduated at Harvard College in 1824, and after studying law was admitted to the Essex bar in 1831. He opened an office in his native town, where he practised but a few years. He was for a considerable period principal of the Newburyport high school; and served several years in both branches of the state legislature. He removed to Boston in 1848, and the next year was appointed by President Taylor United States attorney for Massachusetts. He resigned when the administration was changed, and returned to his practice and the literary work for which he was already famous. He had begun to write and publish poetry at an early age. From 1857 to 1862 he was editor of the *Boston Daily Courier*, the leading democratic paper of

Boston at that time. Upon his retirement from journalism he removed to Scituate, and devoted the remainder of his life to literary pursuits. Being in feeble health, he did comparatively little work beyond occasional contributions, mostly political, to the papers. He was deeply interested in the welfare of the public, and had a wide circle of warm friends. He died in Boston, after an illness of short duration, May 16, 1885, at the age of eighty-one.

Beside several volumes of prose, Mr. Lunt published many poems. His first book was "The Grave of Byron, with other Poems," 1826. His first volume of collected poems appeared in 1839. Then followed "The Age of Gold," 1843, one of his best efforts; "Culture," 1843; "The Dove and the Eagle," 1851; "Lyric Poems, Sonnets and Miscellanies," 1854; "Eastford, or Household Sketches, by Wesley Brooke," 1854; "Julia," 1855; "The Union," 1860; and "Poems," 1884.

HYMN.

SUPPOSED TO HAVE BEEN SUNG BY A CHORUS OF YOUTHS AND MAIDENS AT THE FUNERAL OF BYRON IN GREECE.

O virgin daughters of the budding isles
  Which crowning purple o'er the deep Ægean,
Whose folded foliage met those first-born smiles
  Which made groves, streams, and rocks, sing Io
      Pæan!

Wail, island daughter, him whose day is done,
    And tear the ivy-garland from your head—
Apollo's latest, brightest son
    Is with the mighty dead !

Far-darter of the never-failing bow !
    Healer of nations ! where was then thy power?
Earth called for thee, and why wert thou so slow?
    Or, couldst thou not avert the hour?
Come, father of the morning, come and shake
    Adown thy flowing ringlets' golden store—
But he whom thou didst love to wake
    Shall see thy face no more !

The time of early bloom shall come, and spring
    Anew shall pour her honeydew-fed flowers,
And oft again the vintage months shall bring
    Their purple gifts ; but vernal showers,
Nor summer airs, nor vintage suns shall hail
    His unreturning footstep—for the brave,
The young, the noble whom we wail,
    Is wedded to the grave.

Freedom ! so richly bought, thou shouldst be sweet :
    Yet would that he, thy victim, had but died
Floating down battle's crimson flood to meet
    Red from thy strife the Stygian tide :
How gladly, then, in glory's flowers we'd sheathe
    His sword, and round his consecrated brow
We'd mingle with the poet's wreath
    One deathless laurel bough !

Sons of the Greeks ! 'mid the tumultuous flame
  Of the fierce shock ye shall remember well
Who gave his life, his fortune and his fame,
  Yea, his whole hope, to break the accursed spell
Which ye must end ; but o'er his silent bier,
  Till ancient freedom smiling hovers nigh,
Ye may not waste another tear,
  Or one lamenting sigh.

What though his life was brief ! his young career
  Was run in glory—happy that his last
Act was the best and noblest ; time may sear
  And blight the nations with his withering blast,
But has no power to rend his monument
  From out the hearts of men ; perchance still more
Happy, that he so early went
  Down to the gloomy shore.

But year by year shall Grecian girls renew,
  When spring returns, the story of his woes,
And gather memory's sweetest flowers to strew,
  Violets and lilies and the pale primrose,
For him who slumbers in the orange vale ;
  And often shall Ætolian sires relate,
Weeping, his melancholy tale—
  Their poet-hero's fate !
—1824.

NOTE. Lord Byron went to Greece to assist, by the inspiration of his presence and his song, in securing its freedom in
the war with Turkey. He died there in 1824, at the age of
thirty-six. He was greatly mourned by the Greeks.

8

CAROLINE ATHERTON MASON.

MRS. MASON was born in Marblehead, Mass., July 27, 1823, and was daughter of Dr. Calvin and Rebecca (Monroe) Briggs. She was educated at Bradford Academy. She began to write poetry in her teens, and her first verses appeared in the *Salem Register* over the signature of "Caro." She afterward wrote for the *Anti-Slavery Standard, Commonwealth, The Liberal Christian*, and *National Era*, and later for the *Congregationalist, Independent*, and *Christian Union*, and for *The Century, Monthly Religious Magazine, Scribner's, Lippincott's, St. Nicholas*, and other magazines. She is widely known as the author of "Do They Miss Me at Home?" written while a homesick school-girl, and which was sung by the soldiers at the front throughout the Rebellion. Some of her other songs have been set to music both in this country and in England. She wrote for the Hutchinsons "The Triple-Hued Banner," which they set to music and sang in their concerts throughout the North during the war. Her poetry is imbued with the spirit of the period in which she wrote most. In 1852 the family removed to Fitchburg, and she soon afterward married Charles Mason, Esq., a lawyer of that city, where they have a pleasant home on the side of the famous and picturesque Rollstone Mountain.

Beside a small prose volume, entitled "Rose Hamilton," which was issued by the Massachusetts Sunday-School Society, she published, in 1852, a volume of

poems, entitled, "Utterance, or Private Voices to the
Public Heart, a collection of Home Poems," which she
dedicated to her parents.

WAKING.

I have done at length with dreaming;
  Henceforth, O thou soul of mine,
Thou must take up sword and buckler,
  Waging warfare most divine.

Life is struggle, combat, victory:
  Wherefore have I slumbered on
With my forces all unmarshalled,
  With my weapons all undrawn?

Oh, how many a glorious record
  Had the angels of me kept
Had I done instead of doubted,
  Had I warred instead of wept!

But begone regret, bewailing!
  Ye but weaken like the rest:
I have tried the trusty weapons
  Rusting erst within my breast:

I have wakened to my duty,
  To a knowledge large and deep
That I recked not of aforetime,
  In my long, inglorious sleep.

In this subtle sense of being
    Newly stirred in every vein,
I can feel a throb electric,—
    Pleasure half allied to pain.

'Tis so sweet and yet so awful,
    So bewildering, yet brave,
To be king in every conflict
    Where before I crouched a slave !

'Tis so glorious to be conscious
    Of a growing power within
Stronger than the rallying forces
    Of a charged and marshalled sin !

Never in those old romances
    Felt I half the thrill of life
That I feel within me stirring,
    Standing in this place of strife.

Oh those olden days of dalliance
    When I wantoned with my fate !
When I trifled with a knowledge
    That had well nigh come too late !

Yet, my soul, look not behind thee ;
    Thou hast work to do at last :
Let the brave deeds of the present
    Overarch the crumbled past.

Build thy great aims high and higher ;
    Build them on the conquered sod

Where thy weakness first fell bleeding
And thy first prayer rose to God.
—*1852.*

SUSAN WHITTEMORE MOULTON.

MISS MOULTON was born in Newbury, Mass., in that
portion which is now a part of the city of Newburyport,
June 21, 1856, and was daughter of Hon. Henry William and Susan Floyd (Whittemore) Moulton. She attended the common schools and the Putnam Free
School, supplementing her school education by several
years' private study of English literature, of which she
was excessively fond from childhood. She early wrote
short stories for newspapers and magazines, her first published story being sent to the *Youth's Companion*, at the
age of seventeen. She also sent, from time to time, contributions of poetry, which were well received. At the
age of twenty-two, she wrote the story, entitled "Hill
Rest," which had a large circulation. She recently
spent nearly three years in the South, where she gathered further materials for literary work. She had a slight
figure and was of medium height, with dark hair and
eyes; in conversation she was full of vivacity and intel-
ligence, and very entertaining. Her home was "Moulton
Castle," in Newburyport, on the banks of the Merrimac, the magnificent structure having been erected by
her father about 1861. The views from its towers might
well inspire the most prosaic to the writing of poetic
measure. It was here that Sir Edward Thornton spent

four of the most delightful summers of his life, with the
British Legation, as a lessee of the estate during the ab-
sence of the proprietor who held a government office
in the war.   After a decline of about a year, Miss Moulton died, at her home, February 19, 1889, at the age
of thirty-two.

WILD FLOWERS.

In stately splendor the singer stood,
With the queenly grace of womanhood ;
With higher power than a queen may know,
And greater gifts than a queen may show.
Heavy and hushed grows the waiting air ;
And a sea of faces, dark and fair,
Eagerly lift in the swaying throng,
Waiting the wonderful voice of song.

It comes, and the listeners bend to hear
The soaring melody, grand and clear ;
Till the hour and place and circumstance
Are lost in music's mystical trance.
Breathless the pause and the trembling hush ;
Then, onward and out, with a mighty rush,
Thunders the voice of the raptured throng,
Thrilled and enchained by the power of song !

Like incense wafted from isles of bloom,
Floateth the subtle and rare perfume
Of the royal flowers dropped at her feet,—
Tribute of homage and beauty sweet.

Over the singer's face there came
A swift, bright flush, like a rosy flame;
A smile that gleamed like a glint of dawn,
That riseth over the gates of morn.

Nor triumph nor homage woke that smile,—
Only some flowers from the fragrant pile,
Culled in the dew by a childish hand,
And bashfully flung to the singer grand,—
Only the wildwood flowers that grow
In the sunny glades and valleys low;
Where winds are sweetest, and skies are bright,
And brooklets dance in the golden light.

Higher and higher swells the acclaim;
Tumultuous voices call her name.
Silently yet doth the singer stand,
With only the wild-flowers in her hand.
All unheeded the tribute of cheers,—
Other and distant music she hears;
The singing streams of her native hills,
The pine tree's whisper, and voice of rills.

She sees in fancy the village sward
Beyond the meadow, all daisy-starred;
The laughing brook where the children played,
And the dainty harebells lightly swayed.
She dreams once more in her rocking boat,
Where the cool white lilies idly float;
And the locust blossoms dropping glide
With the summer light on the drifting tide.

And a sudden smile of rarest grace
Swept swiftly over the singer's face ;
With the raptured gaze of one who sees
The far-off fortunate Isles of Peace.
Once more the listening throng is mute,
And, sweeter than voice of harp and lute,
Through aisle and nave to the great arched dome
Ring the magic notes of "Home, sweet home !"

Then the great throng trembled, pulses throbbed,
The voices of careworn worldlings sobbed ;
While prisoned hearts found sweet release
In visions of childhood's home and peace.
And blessings of love and pure content
The humble breath of the wild-flowers sent.

JOHN PATCH.

MR. PATCH was born in Ipswich, Mass., August 23, 1807, and was son of John and Judith (Corning) Patch. He attended Dummer Academy and Phillips Academy, and graduated at Bowdoin College in 1831, being a classmate of the poet Longfellow. He afterward studied Greek and German at Harvard University, subsequently entering the law school, where he graduated in the class with Wendell Phillips and Charles Sumner. He was admitted to the Suffolk bar in 1835, having been for a while in the office of Hon. Theophilus Parsons, in Boston. He immediately opened an office in that city, afterward removing to Nantucket, and later to Beverly. In 1847, he resumed his practice in Boston, and the same year became editor of the *Literary Museum*. In 1849, he went to California as attorney for a Boston company, and, becoming enamored with the climate and magnificent scenery there, took up his abode at San Francisco, where he practised law with fair success until 1853, when he returned to his native town. Before the close of that year his health failed and he again went to California, where he remained until 1856, when he returned to Ipswich to care for his father in his declining years, residing on his father's farm during the remainder of his life. He was passionately fond of nature; and his poetry was similar to Wordsworth's. He was an intelligent writer, a Unitarian in his religious belief, and somewhat eccentric in his habits. He died at his home in Ipswich, after a long illness, September 11, 1887, at the age of eighty.

In 1841, Mr. Patch published a volume of poetry, entitled "The Poet's Offering," which ran through two editions.

LABOR.

Scorn thou not the hands of labor,
　Brawny arms have golden hearts ;
Labor wins the prize of beauty,
　Labor health and strength imparts.

Labor is the key that opens
　Avenues to wealth and fame ;

Labor need not blush, though lowly,
  For to labor brings not shame.

Labor builds the peasant's cottage ;
  Labor rears the palace gate ;
Labor makes the rich more noble,
  And the noble ones more great.

Work, and thou shalt be a brother
  Of the only royal line ;
Work, and thou shalt clothe another,
  Labor makes the soul to shine.

Laborare est orare—
  So the ancient monk declares ;
Laborare est orare
  Echoes from the silent stars.

Industry is life and worship,
  Idleness is guilt and sin ;
Work, and thou shalt feel the presence
  Of the present God within.

Labor is the throne of genius,
  Holiest of holy things ;
Greatest profit, greatest blessing,
  Labor to the laborer brings.

Ye whom, born to wealth and titles,
  Sloth and luxury enthrall ;

Labor and ye shall inherit
Blessings that surpass them all.
—*1847.*

JAMES CHUTE PEABODY.

MR. PEABODY was born in Georgetown, then a part of
the town of Rowley, Mass., February 20, 1828, and was
son of James and Hannah(Chute) Peabody. He spent
his boyhood days at his birthplace, and attended the district school and Dummer Academy. He studied law
in the Harvard law school, and was admitted to the
Suffolk bar. He opened an office, and after a few years'
practice, concluded to enter journalism, relinquishing
his legal profession for which he had displayed considerable talent. He at first went abroad as a newspaper
correspondent. On his return he continued his connection with the press, soon afterward becoming the editor
of the *Newburyport Watchtower*, and subsequently was
employed in the same capacity on the *Newburyport
Weekly Union.* For several years past he has edited
the *Newburyport Daily Germ.* He is also a contributor to other newspapers, and has written both prose and
poetry for *Harper's*, and other magazines. He has
made quite a number of poetical translations from German authors ; and has published a translation of Dante's
"Inferno." He is a ready, brilliant and interesting writer,
and a natural journalist. His poetry is considered ex-
ceptionally good. He still resides in the house in which
he was born in the ancient parish of Byfield.

Mr. Peabody published a volume of his poems, with the title of " Key-Notes," in 1864.

———

THE OLD YEAR AND THE NEW.

Once more old Time unbars the silent tomb,
 In the past land, where his dead years are lying
All side by side, amid the eternal gloom ;
 For now his last-born in the night is dying.

He bids adieu the solemn, dark-robed hours
 That one by one glide by his snowy bed ;
And now the great bells from a thousand towers
 Toll their sad requiem, for the year is dead.

But lo, a new-born cherub, hovering near,
 Whose wings shall sweep the starry circle through !
For the death struggles of the passing year
 Were still the birth pangs of the coming new.

Now Janus wears a smiling face before,
 Yet backward looks a sad, a long adieu ;
From the same fountain doth Aquarius pour
 Tears for the old, libations to the new.

Time buries his dead, and from the tomb comes forth,
 Rolls to the stone, and writes above the door
Another epitaph, that all the earth
 May read and ponder through the evermore.

There is the story of the bygone years,
  Their joys and sorrows, and their love and hate;
And there the lachrymals of bitter tears
  Stand full, forever, by the frowning gate.

There hang the scutcheons of departed nations;
  There glows the red page of their growth and strife,
There lie the ashes of the dead creations;
  A world or creed, a god or mortal life.

And all the legends on those stony pages
  Shall grow to oracles in coming days,
And unborn minstrels, in the unborn ages,
  Shall give them voice in many sounding lays.

Then blot, O Time, the olden error still,—
  All jarring discords from their strains to sever,—
What I have written, be it good or ill,
  That I have written, and it stands forever.

There is no resurrection of the past;
  Its shade may haunt thee, but it lives no more.
Yet mourn it not.   Behold, the future vast,
  The eternal future, stretches on before!

Take, then, the book of fate into thy hand,
  And for the new year write thine own decree;
And what thou writest shall forever stand,
  And what thou willest that the end shall be.

HENRY PICKERING.

MR. PICKERING was born in Newburgh, N. Y., October 8, 1781, and was son of Col. Timothy and Rebecca (White) Pickering. Having a strong desire for city life, his father placed him in a merchant's counting-room in Philadelphia. The position suited his refined mind and manners, and he was happily pursuing his wonted course, when, in his nineteenth year, his father having gone into the wilderness to rear a home, Henry quitted his loved employment and joined him. He never married but consecrated, as it were, his life and service to his father's household. His reverent affection and tender care for his mother were remarkable from childhood. He came to Salem, Mass., and made some adventures in trade, becoming an importer to a considerable amount on his own capital. By his superior business ability, he acquired a large estate. After some years he lost his property, and again entered into business, this time in New York City, where he died, while on a business trip, after a short illness, May 9, 1838, at the age of fifty-six. His mind was highly cultivated by study and foreign travel, and by his association with the best society. His temperament and his mental habits were highly poetic, and his writings were various and spontaneous, being suggested by the contemplation of works of art, and scenes of nature that deeply impressed his imaginative and sensitive spirit. He was genial and cheerful, and fond of young people.

Mr. Pickering published "The Ruins of Pæstum, and Other Compositions in Verse," in 1822 ; "Athens, and Other Poems," in 1824 ; and "Poems, by an American," in 1830.

_____

MORNING.

Light breaks upon the hills ! while through the air
   The spirit of the gale his joyous way
   Wings o'er the land and waters, prompt to pay
To him obeisance. The green woods, where'er
He wends, wave gracefully their tops—nor dare
   The flowers withhold their perfume—nor delay
   The silver-flowing streams, that sparkling play
Along his course, his presence to declare.
But lo ! a visible and mightier power
   Advances in the east, and to a blaze
Kindling the heavens, now rules the fervent hour—
   Earth gladlier smiles in her benignant rays,—
While from the hills, the vales, from every bower,
   Ascends the universal hymn of joy and praise !

—

EVENING.

Wrapped in its broad dark mantle, the dense grove
   Sleeps in the mountain's shadow ; not a breeze
   Plays with the lightest leaf upon the trees,
Or dances on the wave : nor from above
Is longer heard the choral song of love,
   Poured from innumerous little throats to please
   The attentive ear. Each sound, by soft degrees,

With the low cooings of the woodland dove
In silence melts ; while sinking to repose,
   Nature itself is soothed. One last warm gleam
Tinges the distant peaks with blush of rose,—
   And like the magic influence of a dream
Comes o'er the soul—awakening visions there
As beautiful as melancholy fair !

JOHN PIERPONT.

MR. PIERPONT was born in Litchfield, Conn., April 6,
1785, and was son of James and Elizabeth (Collins)
Pierpont. Graduating at Yale College in 1804, he taught
for five years, then studied law, and was admitted to the
bar of Essex county, Mass., in 1812. He practised in
Newburyport until his health failed, when he became a
merchant in Boston, and afterward in Baltimore, where
his business resulted disastrously. He then studied theology, was ordained a Unitarian clergyman, and was pastor of the Hollis street church in Boston from 1819 to
1845, of a church in Troy, N. Y., from 1849 to 1853,
and of another in Medford, Mass., from 1854 to 1856.
He powerfully advocated the temperance and anti-
slavery causes, and served as chaplain in the army.
He published several school readers and many sermons.
He loved nature, cared little for popularity, and lived
for the truth. He had true genius as a poet, and, says
Bungay, "his 'Airs of Palestine,' for sublimity of thought,
beauty of expression, and graceful versification, is un-

excelled by any American production." He was the favorite reform poet of his time in America, among the educated, and probably no other man received so many invitations to read poetry before lyceums as he. During his latter years, he was still erect in figure, with snow-white hair, brilliant, blue eyes, an intellectual forehead, and with a rosy glow of health upon his face. As a speaker he was interesting and eloquent. He died in Medford August 27, 1866, at the age of eighty-one.

Mr. Pierpont published his "Airs of Palestine" in 1816, and his "Airs of Palestine, and Other Poems," in 1840.

THE PILGRIM FATHERS.

The Pilgrim fathers,—where are they?
  The waves that brought them o'er
Still roll in the bay, and throw their spray
  As they break along the shore ;
Still roll in the bay, as they rolled that day
  When the Mayflower moored below,
When the sea around was black with storms,
  And white the shore with snow.

The mists that wrapped the Pilgrim's sleep
  Still brood upon the tide ;
And the rocks yet keep their watch by the deep
  To stay its waves of pride.
But the snow-white sail that he gave to the gale,
  When the heavens looked dark, is gone,—

9

As an angel's wing, through an opening cloud,
　　Is seen, and then withdrawn.

The Pilgrim exile,—sainted name !
　　The hill whose icy brow
Rejoiced, when he came, in the morning's flame,
　　In the morning's flame burns now.
And the moon's cold light, as it lay that night
　　On the hillside and the sea,
Still lies where he laid his houseless head,—
　　But the Pilgrim ! where is he ?

The Pilgrim fathers are at rest :
　　When summer's throned on high,
And the world's warm breast is in verdure drest,
　　Go stand on the hill where they lie.
The earliest ray of the golden day
　　On that hallowed spot is cast ;
And the evening sun, as he leaves the world,
　　Looks kindly on that spot last.

The Pilgrim spirit has not fled :
　　It walks in noon's broad light ;
And it watches the bed of the glorious dead,
　　With the holy stars by night.
It watches the bed of the brave who have bled,
　　And shall guard this ice-bound shore,
Till the waves of the bay, where the Mayflower lay,
　　Shall foam and freeze no more.

ALBERT PIKE.

MR. PIKE was born in Boston, Mass., December 29, 1809, and was son of Benjamin and Sarah (Andrews) Pike. His father, who was a shoemaker, removed his family to Newburyport in 1814. Albert studied for a time at Harvard College, afterward taught school in Newburyport and Fairhaven, and in 1831 went to St. Louis, walking much of the way. He joined an expedition to New Mexico, and became a peddler in Santa Fé. The 'next year he accompanied some trappers, from whom he separated, and walked five hundred miles, reaching Fort Smith, Ark., a stranger without clothing or money. He contributed poetry to the *Arkansas Advocate,* which he afterward edited and owned until 1836, when he was admitted to the bar, to which he devoted himself until 1880. Since that time he has been reading and studying, and attending to his duties as grand-commander of the Masonic order of the South. He has written for periodicals, published legal works and romances, and is entitled to take his place in the highest order of American poets. He resided at Little Rock, Ark., from 1833 to 1865, then at Memphis, Tenn., for three years, and since that time at Washington, D. C., which is his present home. While living at Memphis, he edited the *Memphis Appeal.* He commanded, with distinction, a company of Arkansas Cavalry in the Mexican War ; was also a prominent state-rights advocate, and led a body of Cherokee Indians in the Rebellion, sharing with them the confederates' defeat in the battle of Pea Ridge.

Gen. Pike published "Prose Sketches and Poems" in 1834 ; "Hymns to the Gods" in 1839 ; and a collection of his poems, under the title of "Nugæ," was printed in 1854.

EVERY YEAR.

Life is a count of losses,
 Every year ;
For the weak are heavier crosses,
 Every year ;
Lost springs with sobs replying
Unto weary autumns' sighing,
While those we love are dying,
 Every year.

The days have less of gladness,
 Every year ;
The nights more weight of sadness,
 Every year ;
Fair springs no longer charm us,
The winds and weather harm us,
The threats of death alarm us,
 Every year.

There come new cares and sorrows,
 Every year ;
Dark days and darker morrows,
 Every year ;
The ghosts of dead loves haunt us,
The ghosts of changed friends taunt us,
And disappointments daunt us,
 Every year.

To the past go more dead faces,
  Every year;
As the loved leave vacant places,
  Every year;
Everywhere the sad eyes meet us,
In the evening's dusk they greet us,
And to come to them entreat us,
  Every year.

"You are growing old," they tell us,
  "Every year;
"You are more alone," they tell us,
  "Every year;
"You can win no new affection,
You have only recollection,
Deeper sorrow and dejection,
  Every year."

Too true ! — Life's shores are shifting,
  Every year;
And we are seaward drifting,
  Every year;
Old places, changing, fret us,
The living more forget us,
There are fewer to regret us,
  Every year.

But the truer life draws nigher,
  Every year;
And its morning-star climbs higher,
  Every year;

Earth's hold on us grows slighter,
And the heavy burthen lighter,
And the dawn immortal brighter,
Every year.

MARY NEWMARCH PRESCOTT.

MISS PRESCOTT was a native of Calais, Maine, a
daughter of Joseph Newmarch and Sarah (Bridges)
Prescott, and a sister of Mrs. Harriet Prescott Spofford, the popular authoress.   She entered Pinkerton
Academy in Derry, N. H., at an early age, and afterward attended school for a short time in Newburyport,
Mass., whither her parents had removed, but her education was chiefly under the superintendence of her
oldest sister.   She was still quite young when her first
sketch, a short story, appeared in *Harper's Magazine.*
To *Our Young Folks, Harper's Magazine, Merry's
Museum,* and *Oliver Optic's Magazine* she afterward
contributed a number of stories, whose wit, scenic description, and character delineation, won for them a wide
popularity.   She was very successful, also, in writing
for children ; and a volume of her juvenile stories was
published under the title of " Matt's Follies."   Her
verses were, however, the chief expression of her genius,
and in them her love of nature and power for pathos
had freer play than in other work.   In person she was
tall and slight, blue-eyed, and very fair, her face being
distinguished by an exquisite profile.   In social life her

brilliancy and modesty, her readiness and her drollery, gave her an irresistible charm. Her exceedingly delicate health, which had perhaps prevented the full development of powers that were scarcely surpassed by any of our song writers, culminated shortly after a year of European travel in the brief illness of a swift decline, and she died, in her prime, June 14, 1888, at the home of her brother-in-law, Hon. Richard S Spofford, on Deer Island, Amesbury, Mass.

―――――

ASLEEP.

Sound asleep,—no sigh can reach
  Him who dreams the heavenly dream,
No to-morrow's silver speech
  Wake him with an earthly theme.
Summer rains relentlessly
Patter where his head doth lie,
There the wild fern and the brake
All their summer leisure take,
Violets blinded with the dew
Perfume lend to the sad rue,
Till the day breaks fair and clear
And no shadow doth appear.

―――――

HIRAM RICH.

MR. RICH was born in Gloucester, Mass., October 28, 1832, and was son of Stephen and Nancy (Adams) Rich. He was educated in the private and public schools of his native town, and by the sea-life round about him. With the exception of a few years' residence in Boston and New York City, his life has been spent in his native place. In 1857 he entered the bank of Cape Ann as teller, and in 1865 was appointed cashier of the Cape Ann National Bank, a position which he still holds. He now resides in Gloucester, and devotes himself principally to his bank duties. He is quite well known as a writer of much ability, especially of poetry. He has written more than a score of years for the *Atlantic Monthly*, and has also been a contributor to *Scribner's Magazine, The Independent, Old and New, Lippincott's Magazine*, and other periodicals. His writings are always imbued with the spirit of true poetry. The sky and sea have been a principal inspiration in his efforts, and the foundation of some of his best productions. They are always ready subjects, as his beautiful poem entitled " Before and After" testifies :—

> " Over the blue of the river,
>   Over the barren bay,
> Over the empty islands
>   Cloudland reaches away.
>
> . . . . . .
>
> " Cloudland, mutable cloudland,
>   Lying so far and low,
> Over to thee by daylight
>   My feet unguided go."

COAST-WISE.

Running the chances of shoal and of syren,
 Glare o' the city and glimmer of town,

Mariners we with our hearts in the offing
Sailing the bay up and sailing it down.
Coast-wise and coast-wise, the harbor-lights greet
Down o' the thistle and glimpses of wheat.

Mariners gray in the service of traffic,
Often to venture and rarely to win;
Ever instead of the coveted sea-room
Something to weather the tide setting in.
Coast-wise and coast-wise, the luck o' the lee,
And the breath o' the woodland; but servitors we.

Not for our keel are the seas we would enter;
Not for our deck their illumining spray;
Not for our sails are the touch o' their sunsets.
Oh! for our shallops the wings o' the day!
Coast-wise and coast-wise, the beacon lights clear,
Only to sail the same provinces near!

Nightly in dreams do the syrens delude us,
Blowing us winds that by day-light are gone;
Ever away in the offing are looming,
Continents pink with continual dawn.
Coast-wise and coast-wise, the inlets of song
And the seas, to the singers to whom they belong.

EPES SARGENT.

MR. SARGENT was born in Gloucester, Mass., September 27, 1813, and was son of Capt. Epes and Hannah Dane (Coffin) Sargent. While a school-boy in

Boston, his father took him on a trip to Europe. He was educated at the Boston Latin School and Harvard College. He passed an industrious literary life in New York and Boston, having commenced with his school-boy effusions in *The Literary Journal* and *The Collegian*. He afterward contributed frequently to *The Knickerbocker, Atlantic Monthly, New World*, and other periodicals. He was editor of, or editorially connected with, *The Token, Parley's Magazine, The New England Magazine, Boston Advertiser, Boston Atlas, New York Mirror, New Monthly Magazine, School Monthly*, and *Boston Transcript*, respectively, and also edited several volumes. He prepared a series of popular school books, including speakers and readers, and wrote tales, dramas, biographies, and novels. "Planchette," his famous work on Spiritualism, of which he was one of the best exponents and stanch supporters, appeared in 1869. He wrote of the sea with true poetic and graphic power, and many of his ocean melodies are unexcelled by the efforts of others of a higher reputation. He was also known as a lecturer. He died in Boston December 30, 1880, at the age of sixty-seven.

Mr. Sargent published several volumes of verse, as follows : "Songs of the Sea, and Other Poems," in 1847 ; "Poems," in 1858 ; and "The Woman who Dared," in 1869.

WOODHULL.

'Twas when Long Island's heights beheld
The king's invading horde,

That, by outnumbering foes compelled,
    Our chief gave up his sword.

Then spoke the victor : "Now from me
    No mercy shall you wring,
Unless, base rebel, on your knee,
    You cry, 'God save the king !'"

With reverent but undaunted tone,
    Then Woodhull made reply,—
"No king I own, save one alone,
    The Lord of earth and sky !

"But far from me the wish that ill
    Your monarch should befall ;
So freely, and with right good will,
    I'll say, God save us all !"

Shouted the foeman, "Paltering slave !
    Repeat, without delay,
'God save the king,' nor longer brave
    The fury that can slay !"

But Woodhull said, "Unarmed, I hear ;
    Yet threats cannot appal ;
Ne'er passed these lips the breath of fear,
    And so, God save us all !"

"Then, rebel, rue thy stubborn will,"
    The ruffian victor cried ;
"This weapon shall my threat fulfil ;
    So perish in thy pride !"

Rapid as thought, the murderous blow
  Fell on the prisoner's head ;
With warrior rage he scanned his foe,
  Then, staggering, sank and bled.

But anger vanished with his fall ;
  His heart the wrong forgave :
Dying, he sighed, "God save you all,
  And me, a sinner, save !"

JONATHAN MITCHELL SEWALL.

MR. SEWALL was born at Salem, Mass., in 1748, and
was son of Mitchell and Elizabeth (Price) Sewall. His
parents died in the early part of his life, and he was
adopted by his uncle Chief-Justice Stephen Sewall. He
was apprenticed to mercantile business, but relinquished
it upon being attacked with fever, which reduced him
so low that he took a voyage to Spain for his health.
He was benefited by the trip, but ever afterward had
severe nervous affections. After his return he studied law
with Jonathan Sewall in Boston, and with John Pickering in Portsmouth, N. H., where he was admitted to the
bar, becoming celebrated as a lawyer. He was registrar
of probate for Grafton County, N. H., in 1774, and afterward removed to Portsmouth, where he resided the
remainder of his life. Love of country was a living prin-
ciple with him ; and his eloquence both of tongue and
pen roused the patriotism of the sons of America to
worthiest deeds. He became widely known as a poet,

some of his occasional efforts attaining great popularity, and many of his political songs being published from Maine to Georgia. In 1788, he delivered the "Fourth-of-July Oration" in Portsmouth, which was published. He became addicted to the use of liquor, and for many years previous to his death led an intemperate life. He was eminent in social qualities, being noted for his wit. He died at Portsmouth, after a sickness of about eighteen months, March 29, 1808, at the age of sixty.

Mr. Sewall published in 1798 "The Versification of Washington's Farewell Address;" and a volume of verse, entitled "Miscellaneous Poems," in 1801.

ODE.

FOR THE CELEBRATION OF AMERICAN INDEPENDENCE, 1788.

In the regions of bliss where the Majesty reigns
   Ten thousand bright seraphim shone ;
Winged for flight they all stand, harps of gold in each
         hand,
   When a voice issued mild from the throne.

Ye powers and dominions, bright guardians of realms !
   Whose sway Europe's sons have revered,
Eastern monarchs no more your aid shall implore,
   To the West all your cares be transferred.

That vine which from Egypt to Canaan I brought
   With an out-stretched omnipotent arm,
In Columbia's rich soil from Britannia's bleak isle,
   Shall flourish, and brave every storm.

In vain persecution her wheel shall prepare,
  The tyrant his scourge lift on high ;
The wheel shall be broke, the scourge and the yoke
  All shattered in pieces shall lie.

To accomplish my pleasure, a hero I'll raise,
  Unrivalled in counsel, and might ;
Like the prophet of old, wise, patient and bold,
  Resistless as Joshua in fight.

See the plains of Columbia with banners o'erspread !
  Hark ! the roar of the battle's begun !
Like a sun of the skies, when proud rebels arise,
  He drives the dire hurricane on.

Him terrors, nor treasons, nor dangers shall daunt,
  Till his country, from bondage restored,
Independent and free, all her greatness shall see
  Due alone to his conquering sword.

When the thunder is o'er, and fair peace spreads her
        wings,
  The chief still refulgent shall beam,
Presiding at helm, framing laws for the realm,
  In peace, as in war, still supreme !

When the bright golden age shall triumphant return,
  Millennium's new paradise bloom :
While from earth's distant end, their high state to
        attend,
  All nations with transport shall come !

Hail, America, hail ! the glory of lands !
To thee those high honors are given,
Thy stars still shall blaze till the moon veil her rays,
And the sun lose his pathway in heaven !

HARRIET PRESCOTT SPOFFORD.

MRS. HARRIET ELIZABETH (PRESCOTT) SPOFFORD was a daughter of Joseph Newmarch and Sarah (Bridges) Prescott, and was born in Calais, Me., April 3, 1835. Her parents were both far above the average in mental and moral status. When she was fourteen, her family having removed to Newburyport, Mass., she entered the Putnam Free School in that city, from which she graduated. She afterward pursued studies, including Latin and Greek, in Pinkerton Academy at Derry, N. H., where she completed her school life. At the age of thirty, after an engagement of several years, she was married to Richard S Spofford, Esq., then a law-partner with Caleb Cushing in Newburyport, afterward having his office in New York and Boston. Their only child, a son, died in infancy. With her husband she spent many winters in Washington ; but her home is, and for nearly a score of years has been, on Deer Island, a cosy little spot in the Merrimac river, now included in the town of Amesbury. Mrs. Spofford's literary talent manifested itself quite early. She has written many short stories for the leading periodicals, and has published several volumes of prose. In her best verses, there is

an ease, which, accompanying, as it always does, fresh
and vivid description, produces a delightful effect. One
writer has referred to her as "The American Sappho."
A rare woman among women, Mrs. Spofford is one of
the few of our day who are really noteworthy. She is
modest, gracious and dutiful, with a mind cultivated and
progressive, and a heart hospitable and sympathetic.

A volume of her poems was published in 1882.

VANITY.

The sun comes up and the sun goes down,
   And day and night are the same as one ;
The year grows green and the year grows brown,
   And what is it all, when all is done?
Grains of sombre or shining sand,
Sliding into and out of the hand.

And men go down in ships to the seas,
   And a hundred ships are the same as one ;
And backward and forward blows the breeze,
   And what is it all, when all is done?
Atide with never a shore in sight
Setting steadily on to the night.

The fisher droppeth his net in the stream,
   And a hundred streams are the same as one.
And the maiden dreameth her love-lit dream,
   And what is it all, when all is done?
The net of the fisher the burden breaks,
And always the dreaming the dreamer wakes.

RICHARD S SPOFFORD.

MR. SPOFFORD was the son of Dr. Richard Smith and Frances (Mills) Spofford, and was born in Newburyport, Mass., July 30, 1833. He graduated at the high school in his native place, and attended Dummer Academy, completing his general education at home and abroad under private instruction. He was a good scholar, fond of literature, declamation and debate, and his oratory was pure, graceful and elegant, winning the encomium of Wendell Phillips. Added to his other gifts he possessed poetic genius, and wrote verses of high rank, though a comparatively small number of poems from his pen were published. Mr. Spofford read law, was admitted to the bar, and became the law-partner of Caleb Cushing in Newburyport. He became the private secretary of Mr. Cushing on his appointment as attorney-general of the United States under President Pierce, and accompanied him on his foreign mission. Mr. Spofford won many friends in Washington, where he resided for several years, becoming a favorite at the White House, as also of the leading persons from all parts of the country, and representatives of foreign nations. Later, he had a large law practice in New York, and finally became the private counsellor for a large corporation, having his office in Boston. In 1866, he married Miss Harriet E. Prescott, the authoress. For several years next prior to his decease they resided most of the time at their home on Deer Island in the Merrimac River, in Amesbury, Mass., where he passed

10

away August 11, 1888, at the age of fifty-five, leaving
a memory fraught with true nobleness and generosity to
the poor, whom he esteemed his brethren.

OUR RIVER AND ITS POET.

Long as thy pebbly shores shall keep
    Their tides, O gallant river,
Thy mountain heights to ocean's deep
    Their crystal streams deliver,—

Long as her bugle on thy hills
    The hosts of freedom rallies,
And labor's choral anthem fills
    Thy loveliest of valleys,—

So long thy poet's praise and thine
    Shall live, the years descending;
Thy ripple and his flowing line
    Like song with music blending.

As widens to the waiting sea
    Thy course, by hill and meadow,
So flows his sweet humanity
    Through circling sun and shadow.

While, hallowed thus, no mortal ban
    Unpitying time imposes;
His life who loves his fellow-man
    Wins heaven before it closes.

ANNIE BATCHELDER STEVENS.

MISS STEVENS was born in Salem, Mass., April 12, 1868, and was daughter of Charles Kimball and Mary Elizabeth (Batchelder) Stevens. When she was a year old her parents removed from Salem to Somerville, where she lived nearly sixteen years, and attended the primary, grammar and high schools. In 1884, the family removed to Lynnfield, where she has since resided, enjoying the country, for which she had always longed. She pursued the course of study at the State Normal School in Salem, from which she graduated in 1887, being the poet of her class. She began to write verses at the age of eight, but her poems first appeared in print in the *Radiator*, the Somerville high-school paper, in 1882. Since then she has contributed to the *Salem Gazette, Watchman, Golden Rule, Helping Hand*, and other periodicals. She has also published several stories and papers. Her productions are always meritorious, and she is well worthy of the niche we have given her in this volume, though the youngest of the poets on our list. In reference to her style of writing, she says : " If there is some word I want to speak to any friend or friends, I simply tell it as sweetly as I know how in verse, and that is all." She has always been busy with school and home duties, and is fond of the study of the Bible, believing it to be the foundation of all really beautiful and true knowledge.

GOD'S LOVE.

" He will rest in His love;" or, in the Hebrew, "He will be silent in His love."—ZEPH. III: 17.

I long to speak the beauty rare of yonder sky
Arching in sweet tranquillity.
I long to whisper glowing words when peace descends
And the rich grandeur all the quiet heaven lends,
When sunsets fire the western hill-tops and surround
The earth, and leave the distant mountains jewel-
crowned.

I long to speak the blissful thoughts that rise in me
When all of nature's wealth I see.
But more I long for power to fitly speak of Him,
Who fills my cup of joy unto its utmost brim.
Yet I cannot. Love's jewels lie sometimes too deep
To be upraised to speech. The heart its wealth would
keep.

The life we live, the deeds of truth and beauty shown,
Express the love our hearts have known.
And there are times when hearts indeed are dumb
With love beyond expression, and our spirits come
Into the very presence of our God and hold
Communion with Jehovah in ways manifold.

Yet God loves more than we ; and one day we shall
know
The love unfathomed here below.

Oh, precious thought of his great love ! When God
 hath brought
Home to their joy the loved ones that his grace hath
 sought
He shall be silent in his overwhelming love,
And truly thus shall he its depth and richness prove.

JULIA NOYES STICKNEY.

MRS. STICKNEY was born in West Newbury, Mass.,
July 5, 1830, and was daughter of Somerby Chase
and Mary (Brown) Noyes. Her early childhood was
spent at Newburyport. She attended the academy
at Bradford, and in 1851 was graduated from the Ipswich Seminary. She taught school two years in her
native town, and was principal of the girls' high school
in Haverhill. In 1855, she married Charles Stickney
of Groveland, and became the mother of a large family.
Inheriting her gift from her mother, who left a manu-
script volume of poems, she began to write poetry when
only nine years of age, but discontinued it when she
married. About ten years ago she resumed her literary
work, and has since written much, generally in letters to
papers in Massachusetts, Vermont and New York. She
spends her summers in travelling over picturesque regions, and her winters in Boston, where she has appeared
as a lecturer on her travels and a reciter of her own
poems.

In 1884, she published a small volume of verse, entitled "Poems on Lake Winnipesaukee."

NIGHT, HASTENING FROM THE LAKE.

Was it the soul of night
That charmed my rapturous sight,
Or coming morn, entranced, beyond the wave !
    The crescent moon shone clear,
    The ethereal atmosphere
Was pure with breezes that September gave.

Orion led the band
That lit the shadowy land ;
The royal planets shone on golden throne,
    And all the adoring stars
    Illumed their crystal bars
Till darkness fled and splendor reigned alone.

The auroral, boreal arch
Shone as in skies of March,
That southern skies might shadow back the gleams,
    Vying with Dian clear
    And diamond-dawning, near,
And twilight suns o'er Scandinavian streams.

I saw the mountain lake
The living picture take
Till glowed the heavens with light, translucent, clear,
    That no man's hand may trace,
    Imperial halls to grace,
As earth's grand dream till opening heaven draws near.

ISAAC STORY.

MR. STORY was born in Marblehead, Mass., August 25, 1774, and was son of Rev. Isaac and Rebecca (Bradstreet) Story. He graduated at Harvard University in 1793, and after studying law opened an office, practising first in Castine, Maine, and afterward in Rutland, Mass. While residing at Castine, he edited *The Journal,* which was published there. He was the author of considerable prose, one of his volumes being over the signature of "The Traveller," much of it having first appeared in the *Columbian Centinel.* He wrote in imitation of the celebrated " Peter Pindar," and adopted the *nom de plume* of "Peter Quince." Under this name he published a volume, entitled "The Parnassian Shop," in Boston, in 1801. He wrote popular songs and fugitive pieces, and is generally acknowledged to have been a poet of a good deal of merit. Though dying at so youthful an age he was quite extensively known. He was also an orator of some note, and when quite young participated in public speaking. In 1800 he delivered a eulogy on Washington at Sterling, Mass., where he then resided ; and in 1801 the Fourth-of-July oration at Worcester. The latter address was published, and is still extant. He died in his native town July 19, 1803, when only twenty-eight.

In addition to his prose productions, Mr. Story published in verse "An Epistle from Yarico to Inkle," in 1792 ; and "Consolatory Odes," in 1799.

THE GRAPE.

A SONG.

Come hither, ye sons of good cheer;
  Come hither, and taste of my grape;
'Twill make you old Bacchus revere,
  And the plagues of reflection escape.

It grew on the mountain of joy,
  Was plucked by a foe to dull care;
Its juice can ill nature destroy,
  And light up the brow of despair.

To youth it gives pleasure divine,
  Throws a flush on the pallidest cheek;
The sweetest sensations combine,
  And makes even dumbness to speak.

In age it awakens desire
  For scenes of the purest delight;
Fans to flame lovely Venus' fire,
  And scatters the darkness of night.

Let the hermit reside in his cave,
  And squint at the stars as they rise,
My grape will from solitude save,
  And spangle with stars all your eyes.

Cheer up, then, ye heavy of heart,
  Your sadness and sorrow forbear;
Of my grape, I'll give you a part,
  And dispel all your sorrow and care.

Come, taste it, for time hurries on ;
  Death rattles his bones at your door,
  And the moment will shortly be gone,
    When my grape you can taste of no more.
—*1798.*

JOSEPH STORY.

JUSTICE STORY was born in Marblehead, Mass., September 18, 1779, and was son of Dr. Elisha and Mehitable (Pedrick) Story. He fitted for college at the Marblehead Academy, and in 1798 graduated at Harvard University, where he was distinguished for poetical talent. He studied law, and was admitted to the Essex bar in 1801, beginning practice in Salem. He was a member of congress in 1808 and 1809 ; and in 1811 was appointed, by President Madison, associate-justice of the supreme court of the United States, a position which he held until his death, a period of thirty-four years. For this office he was eminently qualified, and in it he not only won great fame as a judge, but achieved both a European and an American reputation as a jurist. He was a very useful member of the state constitutional convention of 1820. In 1829, he was appointed Dane professor of law in his *alma mater*, and held the position till his death. He received the honorary degree of LL.D. from Harvard, Brown and Dartmouth colleges. He wrote several text books on legal subjects, beside many volumes in the form of decisions, which evince extraordinary learning, luminous exposition, and profound

views of the science of law.   He possessed great collo-
quial powers, and was not easily turned from his opinions.   He died in Cambridge September 10, 1845,
at the age of sixty-five.

When quite young, Mr. Story published a volume of
poems, entitled "The Power of Solitude."   A second
edition was issued in 1804.

The "Life and Letters of Joseph Story," prepared by
his son W. W. Story, was published in two volumes in
1851.

——

ADVICE TO A YOUNG LAWYER.

Whene'er you speak, remember every cause
Stands not on eloquence, but stands on laws—
Pregnant in matter, in expression brief,
Let every sentence stand with bold relief;
On trifling points, nor time, nor talents waste,
A sad offence to learning and to taste ;
Nor deal with pompous phrase ; nor e'er suppose
Poetic flights belong to reasoning prose.
Loose declamation may deceive the crowd,
And seem more striking, as it grows more loud ;
But sober sense rejects it with disdain,
As naught but empty noise, and weak as vain.
The froth of words, the schoolboy's vain parade
Of books and cases—all his stock in trade—
The pert conceits, the cunning tricks and play
Of low attorneys, strung in long array,

The unseemly jest, the petulant reply,
That chatters on, and cares not how, nor why,
Studious, avoid—unworthy themes to scan,
They sink the speaker and disgrace the man.
Like the false lights, by flying shadows cast,
Scarce seen when present, and forgot when past.
Begin with dignity; expound with grace
Each ground of reasoning in its time and place;
Let order reign throughout—each topic touch,
Nor urge its power too little, or too much.
Give each strong thought its most attractive view,
In diction clear, and yet severely true.
And, as the arguments in splendor grow,
Let each reflect its light on all below.
When to the close arrived, make no delays,
By petty flourishes, or verbal plays,
But sum the whole in one deep, solemn strain,
Like a strong current hastening to the main.

— *1833.*

WILLIAM WETMORE STORY.

MR. STORY was born in Salem, Mass., February 19, 1819, and was son of Justice Joseph and Sarah Waldo (Wetmore) Story. He entered Harvard College, from which he graduated in 1838, at the age of nineteen. He pursued a course of legal studies under his father's supervision, and wrote and published several treatises on law subjects. He also published other volumes of prose,

among them being "Roba di Roma," published in
1862, "Graffiti d'Italia," published in 1869, and an ex-
haustive life of his father, which was published in two
volumes in 1851. He was a frequent and entertaining
contributor, in both prose and verse, to the *Boston
Miscellany*. He is a good German scholar, and has
made a number of poetical translations from that language. His poetry is highly esteemed, and ranks among
the best in this country. He is also an accomplished
musician, and widely known as a sculptor. Among the
works of sculpture for which he has become distinguished are busts of Josiah Quincy, James Russell Lowell, and Theodore Parker, and statues of his father and
George Peabody. His "Cleopatra and the Sibyl" and
"Delilah" are much admired. He has resided in Rome,
Italy, since 1848.

Mr. Story published "Nature and Art," the Phi
Beta Kappa poem, which he delivered at Harvard University, in 1844 ; a volume of poetry, entitled "Poems,"
in 1847 ; another volume of poetry in 1856 ; and a poem
entitled "The Roman Lawyer in Jerusalem" in 1870.

MEMORY.

The children of the spirit cannot die !
The sweet affections, trusting childhood knew—
Life's rosy dawn, that filled with sunny dew
The cup of passion, when the heavens were nigh—

The sting of death, which makes our life a sigh—
    These live forever, and their secret hue
    Pervades the air of thought, even as the blue
Fills the deep chamber of the vaulted sky.
Yes, memory forges out its subtle chain
    From every passing act, and thought, and thing,
From the dim past, the echo sounds again,
    If but a careless hand shall touch the string—
As though my spirit thrilled thy casual phrase,
And sound the memories of departed days.

—

SECRET INFLUENCE.

Little we know what secret influence
    A word, a glance, a casual tone may bring,
    That, like the wind's breath on a chorded string,
May thrill the memory, touch the inner sense,
And waken dreams that come we know not whence ;
    Or, like the light touch of a bird's swift wing,
    The lake's still face a moment visiting,
Leaves pulsing rings, when he has vanished thence.
    You looked into my eyes an instant's space,
    And all the boundaries of time and place
Broke down, and far into a world beyond
    Of buried hopes and dreams my soul had sight,
Where dim desires long lost, and memories fond,
    Rose in a soft mirage of tender light.

HARRIET BEECHER STOWE.

MRS. HARRIET ELIZABETH STOWE was born in Litchfield, Conn., June 14, 1812, and was daughter of Rev.
Dr. Lyman and Roxanna (Foote) Beecher. She was
reared in Puritanic simplicity, and attended the academy
in her native place from seven to twelve years of age,
beginning her literary career as a writer for the exhibi-
tions of the academy when in her twelfth year. In 1836,
she married Prof. Calvin E. Stowe. They lived at first
in Cincinnati, Ohio, then removed to Brunswick, Me.,
and afterward to Andover, Mass., where he was a professor in the Theological Seminary. Here they resided
several years. Mrs. Stowe has been very distinguished
and prolific as an author, "Uncle Tom's Cabin," "Dred,"
"The Minister's Wooing," and "Oldtown Folks," being
her best known books. She was co-editor with D. G.
Mitchell of *Hearth and Home* for several years. She
has contributed much to periodicals, her later writings
having been moral tales and stories for the young. Her
style of composition is easy and natural, and her success
is due more to her observation than to her imagination.
She writes when in the mood. She is now a widow, and
continues to reside, in the summer, at her Hartford,
Conn., home, whither they removed from Andover,
and in the winter amid the orange groves of Mandarin,
her Florida estate on the St. John river. She is of medium height, with a slight figure, and a thoughtful face,
full of refinement. Her hair is almost like snow. She

has an easy, unassuming way, and an air of genuine old
New-England domesticity.

Mrs. Stowe published a volume of "Religious Poems"
in 1867.

———

CHRISTIAN PEACE.

When winds are raging o'er the upper ocean,
   And billows wild contend with angry roar,
'Tis said, far down beneath the wild commotion,
   That peaceful stillness reigneth evermore.

Far, far beneath, the noise of tempest dieth,
   And silver waves chime ever peacefully,
And no rude storm, how fierce soe'er he flieth,
   Disturbs the sabbath of that deepest sea.

So to the heart that knows thy love, O Purest,
   There is a temple, sacred evermore,
And all the babble of life's angry voices
   Dies in hushed stillness at its peaceful door.

Far, far away, the roar of passion dieth,
   And loving thoughts rise calm and peacefully,
And no rude storm, how fierce soe'er he flieth,
   Disturbs the soul that dwells, O Lord, in thee.

O, rest of rests ! O, peace serene, eternal !
   Thou ever livest; and thou changest never;
And in the secret of thy presence dwelleth
   Fulness of joy—forever and forever.

WILLIAM BINGHAM TAPPAN.

MR. TAPPAN was born in Beverly, Mass., October 29, 1794, and was son of Samuel and Aurelia (Bingham) Tappan. When William was twelve, his father died, and he was apprenticed to Simon Willard, the Boston clock-maker. In 1815, he went to Philadelphia and set up in the business of clock-making, which he continued about five years. He then, for six years, taught successfully a private academy in Philadelphia. His schooling was very limited, but he had acquired by his earnest efforts a sound education ; and in 1826 he became zealously engaged in Sunday-school work, serving as general agent of the American Sunday-School Union, first in Philadelphia, afterward in Cincinnati, then in Philadelphia again, and from 1838 in Boston, where he remained until his decease, residing with his family at West Needham the last two years of his life. In 1840, he was licensed to preach, and supplied pulpits in and around Boston. He was a fine speaker, having a versatile mind, a thirst for knowledge, and a lifelong desire for the ministry. He was slender in person, with an expressive countenance, deep feelings, a nervous temperament, and was in general genial and social, but at times moody and abstracted. He began to write and publish poetry when quite young. His hymns are much admired, one of the best known beginning

"There is an hour of peaceful rest."

He died, suddenly, of the cholera, at his home in West Needham June 18, 1849, at the age of fifty-four.

Beside his prose works, Mr. Tappan published "New England, and other Poems," 1819; "Poet's Tribute," 1840; "Poems and Lyrics," 1842; " Poetry of the Heart," 1845; " Sacred and Miscellaneous Poems," 1847; " Poetry of Life," 1847; "The Sunday-School, and other Poems," 1848; "Late and Early Poems," 1849; and collections of his poems in 1822, 1834, 1836, and 1848.

WAKE, ISLES OF THE SOUTH.

Wake, Isles of the South ! your redemption is near ;
  No longer repose on the borders of gloom ;
The Strength of His chosen in love will appear,
  And light shall arise on the verge of the tomb.

The billows that gird ye, the wild waves that roar,
  The zephyrs that play when the ocean-storms cease,
Shall bear the rich freight to your desolate shore,
  Shall waft the glad tidings of pardon and peace.

On the islands that sit in the regions of night,
  The lands of despair, to oblivion a prey,
The morning will open with healing and light,
  The glad star of Bethlehem will usher the day.

The altar and idol in dust overthrown,
  The incense forbade that was offered in blood,

11

The priest of Melchizedec there shall atone,
And the shrines of Hawaii be sacred to God !

The heathen will hasten to welcome the time
The day-spring the prophet in vision once saw,
When the beams of Messiah shall gladden each clime,
And the isles of the ocean shall wait for his law.

And thou, Obookiah ! now sainted above,
Wilt rejoice as the heralds their mission disclose ;
And the prayer will be heard, that the land thou didst
       love
May blossom as Sharon, and bud as the rose !
—*1819.*

LYDIA DAVIS THOMSON.

Miss THOMSON, daughter of Peter and Sarah Gerrish
(Davis) Thomson, was born in West Newbury, Mass.,
March 10, 1844. She belongs to a refined and intellectual family, and is of Scotch descent on the paternal
side, her grandfather having been a professor in the university at Edinburgh. At the age of three years, she
removed with her parents to Byfield parish, in the ad-
joining town of Newbury, where she enjoyed a common-
school education. When she was about to enter the
high school, her ill-health, adverse circumstances, and
the sudden death of her father prevented her from pursuing the course that she had marked out for herself.

As she felt able, however, during the years that followed, from time to time she continued her literary advancement alone in her quiet home, and under much difficulty she has secured a position in the world of letters. Most of her writings consist of poetry, of which she has been a great lover from· earliest childhood. She began to rhyme at the age of nine years, and at thirteen constructed her first poem, though she did not publish anything until she was twenty-one. Her printed poems number over two hundred. She has also prepared stories and essays for the papers. She has never married, and has always resided with her mother near the railway station at Byfield, in an unpretentious cottage, devoting most of her leisure hours to literature.

THE BROKEN SONG.

Once, long ago, a deep-toned song I heard,
And sweeter tuned than voice of singing bird,
Or rippling rill, or childhood's ringing mirth ;
　　Aye, richer, deeper, stronger, grander far
Than aught beside I ever heard on earth.

And whether days were right or days were wrong,
Still in my heart I heard the wondrous song,
And in my soul of joy there was no dearth ;
　　But, ah ! one day a discord entered in,
And then the song was like all songs of earth.

Sometimes I eagerly ask : Is it lost?
Or is it I, alone and tempest-tossed,
That cannot hear the sweet song wandering forth?
  Oh, will the heavy sea be ever calm,
That I may hear the song again on earth?

Sometimes, methinks, I catch its low refrain,
But when I listen, lo, 'tis gone again ;
And then my soul this bitter wail sends forth :
  'Tis lost, 'tis lost ! Oh, foolish, vain regret,
The song I heard I'll hear no more on earth.

But I can die ! Oh, blest the boon of death !
For, oh, methinks, when stilled in life's last breath,
I'll hear again those sweet strains pealing forth ;
  In yonder port, where cruel storms ne'er come,
I'll find again the song I lost on earth.
—*August, 1882.*

CYRUS MASON TRACY.

MR. TRACY was a son of Cyrus and Hannah Mason
(Snow) Tracy, and was born at Norwich, Conn., May
7, 1824.   In infancy he contracted a disease, which
developed into severe forms, and in his fifth year took
the shape of an abscess with curvature of the upper
spine.   Through his sixth and seventh years his life was
despaired of, and his health was not regained until his
tenth year, when the disease left a permanent, though

not painful deformity. In October, 1838, he removed to Lynn, Mass., which, with the exception of about two years' residence in Salem, has been his home ever since. He is a great lover of nature and the natural sciences, as well as of the fine arts, especially poetry and music. He has lectured on botanical subjects, and in 1858 published a pamphlet on the flora of Essex county. He is also interested in mechanics, and worked as a cutler and as a finisher in wood and iron seven years. Then until 1855, he was a clerk, and afterward, until 1865, pursued civil-engineering. In 1868 he was elected professor of materia medica and of botany in the Massachusetts College of Pharmacy, at Boston. He retired from the college in 1874, and established a large music school in Lynn, which proved to be unsuccessful. Since then he has given his attention to the duties of a notary public and conveyancer. From 1856 to 1869 he was clerk of the common council of the city of Lynn. Mr. Tracy has devoted much of his life to literature, having been leading writer on the *Lynn Transcript* from 1869 to 1879. He is favorably known as a writer of prose, and as a poet is possessed of much talent.

––––

MONODY.

JAMES BERRY BENSEL.

O weary song-bird, pierced and pained
By poetry, that saw thee chained
And would have set thee free, but strained

The shaft too far—how hast thou gained
Late respite from the slow, deep torture that remained !

For the keen barb, meant to divide
The tether of thy poet-pride,
Although the hand that launched it tried
For that fair use its flight to guide,
Missed that, and sank its point deep in thy quivering
side.

Alas ! poor bird, that still must sing—
Still must thy morning carol bring,
Thine evening melodies outfling—
What strugglings came, thy soul to wring,
Urged by that arrow still that festered 'neath thy wing !

In the dear chant of hope and love,
In the grand hymn of things above,
In flight of eagle, or of dove—
Or whether joy or peace behoove—
How rankled still that thorn that would not e'er remove !

O suffering singer ! shall we mourn
That thy sore heart, so long uptorn,
That thy choked voice, so faint and worn,
Hath ceased at last—hath reached that bourne
Where strong deliverance waits, with golden locks un-
shorn ?

Cruel to bid thee live—to tune
The lyre to melodies of June—

When every stanza, turning soon,
Stung thee, and left its spiteful boon
To smart unseen by night, at morning or at noon.

And so we bid thee rest.   The hand
Of mortal could not this command :
That thou should'st know the breathings bland
Of poet-happiness.   The band
Knotted thy brow too close.   Not this thy promised land.

Rest then.   To thus have gained the shore
Where all that creeps o'er earth's cold floor
Is past, suffice thee well.   No more
The arrow galls.   The laurelled score
Hath thy name, too ; thy sheaf lies ripe beside the door.
—*1886.*

JONES VERY.

MR. VERY was born in Salem, Mass., August 28,
1813, and was son of Capt. Jones and Lydia (Very)
Very.   When a lad, not yet in his teens, Jones made
voyages to Russia and New Orleans with his father, who
was a sea-captain.   When he was eleven years old his
father died, and he worked and earned money with
which to buy books to study.   He graduated at Harvard College in 1836, after only two years' instruction,
ranking second in his class.   He was there appointed a
tutor in Greek, and while performing his duties studied

in the divinity school, which he was compelled to leave before the time for graduating on account of ill health. He returned to Salem in 1838, and was licensed to preach in 1843, but was never ordained, though he occasionally exercised the functions of the office. He was never married, and lived in his native place, with his gifted sisters, in a quiet, unostentatious way. He had a strong spiritual presence, and an almost saintly meekness, combined with an intense love of what was good and true. Into his writings he poured all his soul, and his simple, trusting faith. He possessed an absorbing love of nature, both for its own sake, and because he could see in it the revelation of God to man. He was so much in communion with it that he seemed to lead a lonely existence. The ledgy, barren hills of "Great Pasture" were to him always delightful, and the source of some of his best verses. The sonnet was his favorite poetic style. Bryant commended his poetry for its "extraordinary grace and originality," and pronounced it "among the finest in the language ;" Emerson said that "it bore the unmistakable stamp of grandeur ;" and Matthew Arnold agrees with the other critics, remarking a genuine note not found elsewhere in American poetry. Mr. Very died in Salem, deeply lamented, May 8, 1880, at the age of sixty-six.

His works have been published as follows : "Essays and Poems," in 1839 ; "Poems," with an introductory memoir by Wm. P. Andrews, in 1883 ; and "Poems and Essays," with portrait, and a biographical sketch by James Freeman Clarke, in 1886.

THE SON.

Father, I wait thy word. The sun doth stand
  Beneath the mingling line of night and day,
A listening servant, waiting thy command
  To roll rejoicing on its silent way;
The tongue of time abides the appointed hour,
  Till on our ear its solemn warnings fall;
The heavy cloud withholds the pelting shower,
  Then every drop speeds onward at thy call;
The bird reposes on the yielding bough,
  With breast unswollen by the tide of song;
So does my spirit wait thy presence now
  To pour thy praise in quickening life along,
Chiding with voice divine man's lengthened sleep,
While round the Unuttered Word and Love their vigils
    keep.

—

NATURE.

Nature! my love for thee is deeper far
  Than strength of words, though spirit-born, can tell;
For while I gaze they seem my soul to bar,
  That in thy widening streams would onward swell,
Bearing thy mirrored beauty on its breast,—
  Now, through thy lonely haunts unseen to glide,
A motion that scarce knows itself from rest,
  With pictured flowers and branches on its tide;
Then, by the noisy city's frowning wall,
  Whose arméd heights within its waters gleam,

To rush with answering voice to ocean's call,
    And mingle with the deep its swollen stream,
Whose boundless bosom's calm alone can hold
That heaven of glory in thy skies unrolled.

LYDIA LOUISA ANN VERY.

Miss Very was born in Salem, Mass., November 2, 1823, and was daughter of Capt. Jones and Lydia (Very) Very. She has always resided in her native city with her sister and brothers, the latter being now deceased, and was for more than thirty years a teacher in the public schools there. She shares largely in the fine poetic gift which distinguishes the family, and is admired for her natural grace, fine fancy, and delicacy of observation, as exhibited in her productions, being well-known as a poetess throughout New England. She has an ease of versification, and a freedom from tricks of style and mannerism which cover up shallow thoughts with deep-sounding words. She writes because she has something to say. The religious sentiment is strong in her nature, and her poems inspired thereby are the most valued. Some of these are very striking in idea and beautiful in expression. In others of her poems, owing to the difficulty of finding sufficiently fitting language, the thought is more poetic than the expression. Some of her sweetest lines are wrought from her love of little children and of nature. For many years she has contributed to the Boston and Salem papers, in both prose and verse.

She is also an artist, and has produced pictorial illustrations of "Red Riding Hood," and other children's stories, accompanied by exquisite designs and pretty juvenile verses. These have proved to be very popular, and have been republished in Germany.

Miss Very published a volume of verse, entitled "Poems," in 1856.

———

LINES.

The foot-crushed flower fresh fragrance yields;
  The dying bird more sweetly sings;
The trampled hay perfumes the fields;
  And from a harp the wild wind brings
Sweet notes of melody, as softly played
As if an angel's fingers o'er it strayed.

And spirits crushed by weight of care,
  Bent by neglect like broken reeds,
Whose burdens are too hard to bear,
  Have filled the world with mighty deeds;
Thus sorrow rudely striking the heart's strings
Forth from the trembling chords sweet music brings.

Genius hath found its noblest sons
  Among the long despised, the poor!
Amid earth's meek and lowly ones,
  Whose powers expand as they endure!
Crushed 'neath the iron heel of haughty pride,
Heart perfume springeth where the mind's flowers hide.

Many a blow the gem must bear,
　Ere it to us appears a gem ;
Earth must its chilling garment wear,
　Its icy crown as diadem,
Ere from its lap the shining blades can spring
And it to man a golden harvest bring !

The spirit cold neglect must feel,
　Earth's crown of thorns its brow must wear ;
Ere from the mind a thought can steal,
　Or it with kindred minds can share
The calm enjoyment of those noble powers,
Which find in heaven the fruit of earth's pale flowers.

ELIZABETH STUART PHELPS WARD.

Mrs. Ward was born in Boston, Mass., August 31, 1844, and was the daughter of Professor Austin and Elizabeth (Stuart) Phelps. Her early life was spent in Andover, Mass., her father having been one of the professors in the theological seminary there for several years. Andover has been Mrs. Ward's home, though much of her summers has been spent at East Gloucester, on Cape Ann, until her marriage with Rev. Herbert D. Ward of New York October 20, 1888. She began to write for publication quite early in life, and has since devoted herself to her literary work, having published many story books. There have been issued in all twenty-nine volumes of her fiction, and some of them, such as "Gates

Ajar," have been remarkably successful in their sales. She has been a contributor to *Harper's Magazine, Our Young Folks, Atlantic Monthly, Independent,* and other periodicals. Beside her prose works she has written considerable verse. Some of her poems have a despondent cast, being pervaded by a mystical, dreamy thoughtfulness; others are bright and witty, betokening a happy and contented frame of mind; and all contain certain varied beauties. She has accomplished much for one who is in delicate health.

Mrs. Ward is the author of "Poetic Studies," a volume of poems published in Boston in 1875; and also of "Songs of the Silent World, and Other Poems," which appeared in 1885.

————

DO I LOVE YOU?

Do I love you? Do I love you?
Ask the heavens that bend above you
To find language and to prove you
    If they love the living sun.
Ask the burning, blinded meadows,
What they think about the shadows,
If they love the falling shadows,
    When the fervid day is done.

Ask the bluebells and the daisies,
Lost amid the hot field-mazes,
Lifting up their thirsty faces,
    If they love the summer rains.

Ask the linnets and the plovers,
In the nest-life made for lovers,
Ask the bees, and ask the clovers—
    Will they tell you for your pains?

Do I, darling, do I love you?
What, I pray, can that behoove you?
How in love's name can I move you,
    When for love's sake I am dumb?
If I told you, if I told you,
Would that keep you, would that hold you,
Here at last where I enfold you?
    If it would—Hush! darling, come!

MARY ANN WEBBER.

MRS. WEBBER was born in Beverly, Mass., February 22, 1823, and was daughter of Israel and Polly (Wallis) Trask. She attended Bradford Academy for a short time, and received the remainder of her education in the private schools that existed in her native town at that period. She married Ezekiel W. Webber of Beverly, who died in 1856, and she remained his widow. She was possessed of a fine poetic talent, which she exercised to a considerable extent, and might have used more freely had she been less modest. She wrote for some time under the *nom de plume* of "Mary Webb," but learning that another writer was using the same name she dropped it, and afterward published her efforts anonymously. During the latter years of her life she printed very little, but wrote from time to time for her own amusement and the entertainment of her friends. Her poems were mostly occasional, and were written for the *Telegraph, Boston Atlas, Salem Gazette,* and other newspapers. In 1861, with Mrs. Phebe A. Hanaford, she was engaged in compiling a little volume of patriotic verses under the title of " Chimes of Freedom and Union," to which she contributed. She died of pneumonia, at her home in Beverly, where she always resided, March 25, 1889, at the age of sixty-six.

———

THE TRAITOR'S THREAT.

"We will march to the tomb of Washington."—*Alexander H. Stephens.*

Hold back your breath, ye breezes
That oversweep the mound,
Within whose precincts is the dust
That hallows Vernon's ground.

Refuse your echoes, lest they waft
The mutterings dark and deep,
Whose lightest whisper would disturb
The honored patriot's sleep.

Let winter's icy touch restrain
The balmy zephyr's wing,
Waking to life the germs that wrap
The verdure of the spring.

For like the serpent's trail, amid
  The early Eden bloom,
Would be the traitor's crest 'mid flowers
  That blossom round that tomb.

Thou broad Potomac, bid thy waves
  O'erflood their ancient bed,
And thus exempt the sacred soil
  From the insurgent's tread !

And if a darker wave must flow,
  To guard that holy spot,
In freedom's name, my countrymen !
  Withhold, withhold it not.

God has decreed that it shall bear,
  Upon its bloody crest,
The ark of freedom, till it reach
  An Ararat of rest.

—*1863.*

ANNA MARIA WELLS.

MRS. WELLS was born in Gloucester, Mass., in 1795, and was daughter of Benjamin and Mary (Ingersoll) Foster. Her father died when she was about four years of age, and her mother married Joseph Locke, a merchant of Boston, whither she removed, making that city her permanent home. The daughter was thoroughly educated ; and, in 1821, became the wife of Thomas

Wells of Boston, an author of much reputation, an offi-
cer of the United States revenue service, and a grandson of the patriot Samuel Adams. Mrs. Wells' chief
attention was given to her school for young ladies. She
began to write when very young, but published little
until her marriage. Her poetry like her themes, which
were generally those suggested by the country, was simple, pure and fervent. She wrote for the *Overland
Monthly, Ladies' Magazine, Our Young Folks,* and
other periodicals of her time. She had great personal
beauty, and graceful manners. Possessed of remarkable conversational powers, her thoughts and words being full and bright, she enjoyed the society of Emerson, Holmes, Longfellow, and other great minds. She
was generous and loving, and was loved by all who knew
her. Poetry showed itself not only in words and in the
loveliness of her person and character, but also in her
talent for music and painting. She died in Roxbury,
Mass., December 19, 1868, at the age of seventy-three,
and lies at rest in the beautiful Forest Hills.

Mrs. Wells published a volume, entitled " Poems and
Juvenile Sketches," in 1831.

MORNING.

Of all his starry honors shorn,
    Away old night is stealing ;
And upward springs the laughing morn,
    A joyous life revealing.

12

Blue-eyed she comes with tresses spread,
   And breath than incense sweeter;
The mountains glow beneath her tread,
   Light clouds float on to meet her.

The tall corn briskly stirs its sheaves;
   A thousand buds have burst
The soft green calyx, that their leaves
   To greet her may be first.

The flowers, that lay all night in tears,
   Look upward one by one;
And pearls each tiny petal bears,
   An offering to the sun.

With beads the trembling grass is dressed,—
   Each thin spire hath its string,
Scattered in mist, as from her nest
   The ground-bird flaps her wing.

The lake obeys the zephyr's will,
   While, as by fingers pressed,
The bending locust buds distil
   Their sweetness o'er its breast.

With busy sounds the valley rings;
   The ploughman yokes his team;
The fisher trims his light boat's wings,
   And skims the brightening stream.

The gentle kine forsake the shed,
   And wait the milk-maid's call;

The frighted squirrel hears her tread,
And scuds along the wall.

Scattering the night clouds as in scorning,
Bright pour the new-born rays ;
There's more of life in one sweet morning,
Than in a thousand days.

––––––

JOHN GREENLEAF WHITTIER.

MR. WHITTIER, "the Quaker poet," was born in Haverhill, Mass., December 17, 1807, and was son of John
and Abigail (Hussey) Whittier.   In early life he worked
on his father's farm, and had about twelve weeks of
schooling in the year.   At the age of eighteen he spent
two terms at the academy in his native town.   In 1836,
he removed with the family to Amesbury, which has
since been his permanent home, although for several
years past he has resided much of the time at "Oak
Knoll," his beautiful country seat at Danvers.   In 1829,
he became editor of the *American Manufacturer*, and
afterward of the *Essex Gazette, Middlesex Standard,
Pennsylvania Freeman, Anti-Slavery Reporter*, and *National Era.*   He was a member of the State legislature
in 1835, and became one of the foremost champions of
the cause of the slave.   He is a Quaker,—unassuming,
accessible and frank.   Some have called him liberal in
his religious belief, and so he is ; but his freedom is that
of truth and love as manifested in God.   When in his

prime he was tall and slender, with black hair and large, black eyes, glowing with expression. His black eyes still sparkle, but he is a little bent, and his hair is gray. His poems are particularly the literature of the common people, for whom they were written, and the offspring of his own beautiful simplicity, "Snow-Bound" being one of his best productions. He has never married.

Beside the editing of several works, Mr. Whittier has published a number of prose volumes of his own composition. He is best known, however, by his poetical works, which are "Legends of New England," 1832; "Moll Pitcher," 1832; "Mogg Megone," 1836; "The Bridal of Pennacook;" "The Voices of Freedom," 1841; "Lays of My Home, and Other Poems," 1843; "Songs of Labor, and Other Poems," 1848; "The Chapel of the Hermits, and Other Poems," 1852; "A Sabbath Scene," 1854; "The Panorama, and Other Poems," 1856; "Home Ballads and Poems," 1859; "In War Time," 1863; "Snow-Bound," 1865; "National Lyrics," 1865; "Maud Müller," 1866; "Tent on the Beach," 1867; "Among the Hills," 1868; "Ballads of New England," 1869; "Miriam," 1870; and several complete collections of his poems.

THE ETERNAL GOODNESS.

O friends ! with whom my feet have trod
    The quiet aisles of prayer,
Glad witness to your zeal for God
    And love of man I bear.

I trace your lines of argument ;
   Your logic linked and strong
I weigh as one who dreads dissent,
   And fears a doubt as wrong.

But still my human hands are weak
   To hold your iron creeds :
Against the words ye bid me speak
   My heart within me pleads.

Who fathoms the Eternal Thought ?
   Who talks of scheme and plan ?
The Lord is God ! He needeth not
   The poor device of man.

I walk with bare, hushed feet the ground
   Ye tread with boldness shod ;
I dare not fix with mete and bound
   The love and power of God.

Ye praise his justice ; even such
   His pitying love I deem :
Ye seek a king ; I fain would touch
   The robe that hath no seam.

Ye see the curse which overbroods
   A world of pain and loss ;
I hear our Lord's beatitudes
   And prayer upon the cross.

More than your schoolmen teach, within
   Myself, alas ! I know :

Too dark ye cannot paint the sin,
　　Too small the merit show.

I bow my forehead to the dust,
　　I veil mine eyes for shame,
And urge, in trembling self-distrust,
　　A prayer without a claim.

I see the wrong that round me lies,
　　I feel the guilt within ;
I hear, with groan and travail-cries,
　　The world confess its sin.

Yet, in the maddening maze of things,
　　And tossed by storm and flood,
To one fixed trust my spirit clings ;
　　I know that God is good !

Not mine to look where cherubim
　　And seraphs may not see,
But nothing can be good in Him
　　Which evil is in me.

The wrong that pains my soul below
　　I dare not throne above :
I know not of His hate,— I know
　　His goodness and His love.

I dimly guess from blessings known
　　Of greater out of sight,
And, with the chastened Psalmist, own
　　His judgments too are right.

I long for household voices gone,
  For vanished smiles I long,
But God hath led my dear ones on,
  And he can do no wrong.

I know not what the future hath
  Of marvel or surprise,
Assured alone that life and death
  His mercy underlies.

And if my heart and flesh are weak
  To bear an untried pain,
The bruised reed he will not break,
  But strengthen and sustain.

No offering of my own I have,
  Nor works my faith to prove ;
I can but give the gifts he gave,
  And plead his love for love.

And so beside the Silent Sea
  I wait the muffled oar ;
No harm from him can come to me
  On ocean or on shore.

I know not where his islands lift
  Their fronded palms in air ;
I only know I cannot drift
  Beyond his love and care.

O brothers ! if my faith is vain,
  If hopes like these betray,

Pray for me that my feet may gain
The sure and safer way.

And thou, O Lord ! by whom are seen
Thy creatures as they be,
Forgive me if too close I lean
My human heart on thee !

HIRAM OZIAS WILEY.

Mr. Wiley was born in Middlebury, Vt., May 20,
1831, and was son of Phineas and Mary (Ellis) Wiley.
He came to Danvers, Mass., when about sixteen years
of age, and was there employed in the manufacture of
shoes for several years.   His mental qualities would not
permit him to while away his life in the humdrum oc-
cupation of a shoemaker.   He felt an irresistible desire
for a different and more intellectual existence.   He concluded to become a lawyer, and after pursuing the necessary studies was admitted to the Essex bar in 1855,
opening an office in that part of Danvers, which was in-
corporated as South Danvers (now Peabody) the same
year.   He afterward resided in Lynn a short time, and
returned to Peabody, where he lived during the remainder of his life, having a limited practice.   He
gave a large portion of his time and thought to literature, being for a few years editor of the *Essex States-
man.*   He wrote considerable verse, some of his poems
being fine, and most of them partaking of the spirit of

his despondent, unsuccessful life, which led him to ex-
claim,

> "O Life! is thy large promise vain
> Of ripened shocks, of bearded grain?
> Do thy hard husks no fruit contain?"

He sought to drown his sorrows and cares in the exhil-
arating cup, and became a wreck in his prime. In very
destitute circumstances, he died of the small pox, in Peabody, January 28, 1873, at the age of forty-one. His
social qualities won for him many friends, who often re-
lieved his impecuniosity. He had a generous, humorous disposition.

A volume of Mr. Wiley's poems was published in
1874, it being entitled "Eternity, and Other Poems."

THE POOR ATTORNEY.

Morn and evening, in an easy chair
 Sits an attorney sadly musing;
Morn, noon and evening, sitting there,
 Blackstone, Coke, and Littleton perusing,
  With an air
Of anxious waiting, in his easy chair.

Boots unpolished, and cravat awry,
 Feet exalted on a dingy table,
Coat undusted, and a dreamy eye;
 Talk of fees to him seems all a fable.
  "By and by!"
He, uprising, mutters, with a sigh.

Morn, and noon, and evening, " Well-a-day ! "
  It is strange that modest merit never
Did succeed, as all old people say
  It never did ; though so very clever,
      He for aye
Must wait till every dog has had his day.

There he sits, with hand beneath his chin,
  Hears the wind about the casements humming ;
Hopes, to cheer him, some one may drop in,
  Wonders when the good time is a-coming.
      Pale and thin,
Sits there with his hand beneath his chin.

Dreams he has dreamed till he is gray,
  Each dream has in its turn betrayed him,
And their ghosts seem mockingly to say,
  " Ample propositions hope once made him."
      Law's delay
Has turned the poor attorney gray.

So he sits there ; the good God doth know
  How his rent and tailor's bills he's paying ;
Ne'er on him did prosperous breezes blow,
  Or swell his sails, while he a-wanton straying :
      Why 'tis so,
Poor attorney, the good God doth know.

So he sits there ; let us hope that still
  " They also serve who only stand and wait ; "
Who "shapes our ends, rough hew them as we will,"

The partial goddess, fortune called, or fate,
Yet may fill
His cup with good, although he sitteth still.

WILLIAM WINTER.

MR. WINTER was born in Gloucester, Mass., July 15, 1836, and was son of Charles and Louisa (Wharf) Winter. His mother, who was the daughter of an Italian, died when he was four years of age. He was educated in the schools of Gloucester, Boston and Cambridge, took a degree at Harvard College, and in Dane Law School, and was admitted to the bar, but never practised. He lived in Gloucester and Cambridge, and removed, in 1860, to New York, where he still resides. He had five children, one of whom died in 1886, and in his memory Mr. Winter founded "The Arthur Winter Memorial Library" in the Staten Island Academy and Latin School, at Stapleton. His years have been passed in hard work. He has tried to make life sweet and gentle for other people ; and his productions have honored truth and virtue. He has written many books, and has added to the poetic literature of his native land by his rich imagination and his cultivated talent, having contributed to the *New York Tribune, New York Albion, Atlantic Monthly, Home Journal, Boston Transcript*, and other magazines and journals ; and having edited two volumes of George Arnold's poems. He has been the dramatic critic for the *New York Tribune*

since August, 1865, and has always advocated a noble
stage.   In the streets of New York City he attracts attention by his venerable appearance and his flowing
snow-white hair.

Beside Mr. Winter's prose works he has published
several volumes of poems: "The Convent, and Other
Poems" in 1854; "The Queen's Domain, and Other
Poems" in 1858; and "My Witness" in 1871.

THE ANGEL DEATH.

Come with a smile, when come thou must,
    Evangel of the world to be,
And touch and glorify this dust—
    This shuddering dust, that now is me—
    And from this prison set me free !

Long in those awful eyes I quail,
    That gaze across the grim profound :
Upon that sea there is no sail,
    Nor any light, nor any sound
    From the far shore that girds it round.

Only—two still and steady rays
    That those twin orbs of doom o'ertop ;
Only—a quiet, patient gaze
    That drinks my being drop by drop,
    And bids the pulse of nature stop.

Come with a smile, auspicious friend,
    To usher in the eternal day !

Of these weak terrors make an end,
   And charm the paltry chains away
That bind me to this timorous clay !

And let me know my soul akin
   To sunrise, and the winds of morn,
And every grandeur that has been
   Since this all-glorious world was born,—
   Nor longer droop in my own scorn.

Come when the way grows dark and chill !
   Come when the baffled mind is weak,
And in the heart that voice is still,
   Which used in happier days to speak,
   Or only whispers, sadly meek.

Come with a smile that dims the sun !
   With pitying heart and gentle hand !
And waft me from my vigil done,
   To peace, that waits on thy command,
   In some mysterious better land.

GEORGE EDWARD WOODBERRY.

MR. WOODBERRY was born in Beverly, Mass., May 12, 1855, and was son of Henry Eliot and Sarah Dane (Tuck) Woodberry. He received his education at Phillips' Academy in Exeter, N. H., and at Harvard College, graduating from the latter institution in 1877. He was a professor of English literature in the State

University of Nebraska in 1877 and 1878, and also from 1880 to 1882. In 1878 and 1879 he was on the editorial staff of *The Nation*, and for the last year has been attached to the *Boston Post*. He has contributed to *The Nation* and the *Atlantic Monthly* regularly for several years, and occasionally to other periodicals. He has written a " History of Wood Engraving," published by the Harpers in 1883 ; " The North-Shore Watch, a Threnody," privately printed in 1883 ; and "Life of Edgar Allen Poe" in the " American Men of Letters," published in 1885. As a poet, Mr. Woodberry stands very high with the scholars and critics of our land, many believing him to be the coming American poet. He has published but few poems, and probably their number will never be great. His production entitled " My Country," which is so widely and favorably known for its patriotic language, was set to music by Prof. John K. Paine, and brought out at the recent Cincinnati festival. In 1885, Mr. Woodberry spent some months in Italy, and passed the winter of 1888-9 in Europe. He resides in his native town, and devotes his time to literary work.

———

AT GIBRALTAR.

I

England, I stand on thy imperial ground,
   Not all a stranger ; as thy bugles blow,
   I feel within my blood old battles flow,—

The blood whose ancient founts in thee are found.
Still surging dark against the Christian bound
    Wide Islam presses ; well its peoples know
    Thy heights that watch them wandering below ;
I think how Lucknow heard their gathering sound.

I turn, and meet the cruel, turbaned face ;
    England, 'tis sweet to be so much thy son !
I feel the conqueror in my blood and race ;
    Last night Trafalgar awed me, and to-day
Gibraltar wakened ; hark, thy evening gun
    Startles the desert over Africa !

II

Thou art the rock of empire, set mid-seas
    Between the East and West, that God has built ;
    Advance thy Roman borders where thou wilt,
While run thy armies true with his decrees.
Law, justice, liberty, — great gifts are these ;
    Watch that they spread where English blood is
        spilt,
    Lest, mixed and sullied with his country's guilt,
The soldier's life-stream flow, and Heaven displease.

Two swords there are : one naked, apt to smite,
    Thy blade of war ; and, battle-storied, one
Rejoices in the sheath, and hides from light.
    American I am ; would wars were done !
Now, westward, look, my country bids good-night,—
    Peace to the world from ports without a gun.

KATE TANNATT WOODS.

MRS. WOODS was born at Peekskill, N. Y., December
29, 1840, and was daughter of James Sullivan and
Mary (Gilmour) Tannatt.   Her father was an editor,
and her mother was one of the famous Scotch Gilmour
family near Edinburgh, whose old castle of Craigmillar
is still owned by descendants of Sir John Gilmour,
once a favorite writer for the *Signet.*   Mrs. Woods was
a delicate child. She attended the seminary in her native town, and also had private instruction. Her father
died about 1850, and the rest of the family left their
home by the Hudson, and removed to Salem, Mass.
While yet in her teens she married George Henry
Woods, Esq., a Salem gentleman, who was at that time
conducting a prosperous law business at Minneap-
olis, Minn.   The Rebellion broke out and he became
a colonel in the army, where he was so seriously in-
jured that he could do no more business. Mrs. Woods,
who had published articles since ten years of age, then
supported the family by her pen. She has written constantly for many years, contributing to the *St. Paul Pio-
neer,* the Omaha papers, and to many New England
papers.   Her poems, stories and books are all pure,
sweet and strong. Her juvenile stories in *St. Nicholas,*
Wide Awake, and other periodicals are popular with
the young people, and her editorial work in the *Boston
Globe* and *American Home Magazine* is clear, terse
and vigorous. She is the author of several dialect poems, which are widely quoted. She also uses the

brush.   Her husband died several years ago, and she
has since resided in Salem.

———

AN INCIDENT OF THE CIVIL WAR.

On my finger I've a token
    Of the long ago,
Days when vows were seldom broken,
When love lived, though oft unspoken,
When war reigned on land and sea,
Then this token came to me.

He who wore it died in battle
    In the long ago ;
'Midst the shot, and 'midst the shell,
His weak voice could only tell,
"Sergeant, when my friend you see,
Give this ring, and speak of me."

So the sergeant took the circle,
    Worn so long ago ;
And through years of weary waiting,
Hope now growing, now abating,
Then he found and gave it me,
The inscription plain to see :
    "As I love, love me."

Soldier brave and soldier young,
    In the long ago ;
Thy sad story shall be sung,

13

How thy heart with sorrow wrung ;
Cherished still, his tender token,
With its love-note softly spoken.

Bride of weeks and bride of death,
    In the long ago ;
Loving me with his last breath,
No rude hand must touch the ring,
No coarse voice his sorrow sing,
Only one both loved must see
    "As I love, love me."

So the little token found me
    In the long ago ;
Worn the gold, the motto clearer,
As the years come near and nearer,
And the lost ones seem still dearer.
Love has grown by faith to see
All the meaning there may be
In the note so sadly spoken,
In the golden band unbroken :
    "As I love, love me."
—1887.

OTHER POETS.

Of some of our writers complete sketches were not
obtained, and others were learned of too late for inser-
tion in their proper places. These are included among
those that follow.

The Rev. JOSEPH CAPEN, born at Dorchester in 1658, minister at Topsfield from 1682 to his decease in 1725, was a writer of verse, and author of an epitaph on John Foster, the printer of the seventeenth century. Rev. NICHOLAS NOYES of Salem also wrote poetry about 1708. So did Rev. JOHN BARNARD, minister at Marblehead, who was born in 1681, and died in 1770. Dr. JOSEPH ORNE, a native of Salem, who was born in 1747 and died in 1786, was a physician in Beverly, and had a fine and poetic mind, but wrote very little. Rev. LEVI FRISBIE, minister at Ipswich from 1776 to his death, which occurred in 1806, wrote some poetry; as also did his son Prof. LEVI FRISBIE, who was born at Ipswich in 1784. Rev. SAMUEL WORCESTER of Salem, who was born at Hollis, N. H., in 1770, and died in 1821, wrote hymns at the beginning of this century. WILLIAM BIGELOW, who graduated at Harvard College in 1794, was a resident of Salem, where he taught school a number of years, and died in 1844, at the age of seventy, having published "Education," a poem, at Salem in 1799; "*Phi Beta Kappa,*" a poem, in 1811; and a "Poem on Intemperance" in 1834. ENOCH MUDGE, who was born at Lynn in 1776, and who died there in 1850, wrote some instructive and admonitory poetry. He published "Lynn; a Poem," in pamphlet form, in 1826. Dr. ANDREW NICHOLS, who was born at Danvers in 1785, and died there in 1853, having practised medicine for many years, wrote occasional poems and hymns. He was in the habit of writing a poem every Sunday. NATHANIEL LORD, jr., of Ipswich, sometimes indulged in rhyme and measure. Rev. JAMES FLINT, a native of Reading, was pastor of the East church in Salem from 1825 to 1851, and wrote many occasional poems and hymns, publishing a volume of poetry in 1852. He was also principal of Bradford Academy for a while. Rev. JOHN W. HANSON wrote for the local papers while he was settled in Danvers some forty years ago. FREDERICK KNIGHT, brother of Rev. Henry C. Knight, was born at Hampton, N. H., in 1791, and spent nearly the whole of his life at Rowley, Mass., where he died in 1849, having written considerably in metre. He was educated at Harvard College, and at the Litchfield, Conn., Law School. Some of his poems are found in his memorial volume, entitled "Thorn-Cottage, or the Poet's Home," published in 1857, in one of which are found the following lines :—

> "While shallow brooks and slender rills,
>   Derived from rains and little hills,
>   Go tinkling on their way
>   As if they thought their noisy thanks
>   Would please the springs along their banks,
>   As shallow things as they;
> *Deep rivers*, by the mountains fed,
>   Exhaustless as their fountain-head,
>   Roll silent to the sea."

He gave all of his manuscripts and those of his brother Henry (which had become his property) to Miss Elizabeth Wheelwright of Newburyport, who had been, as he said in his will, "a ministering angel of mercy" to him. ENOCH CURTIN, a shoemaker, who was born at Lynn in

1794, and died in 1842, resided in his native town, and
had considerable poetic talent, but no ambition to de-
velop it. He wrote occasional odes and songs. The
distinguished historian WILLIAM HICKLING PRESCOTT,
who was born at Salem in 1796, published a " Scotch
Song," and two books on Italian poetry. Mrs. LAVINIA
WESTON of Georgetown, her native place, who is now
eighty-nine years of age, has written and still writes
hymns of good quality. The Hon. CALEB CUSHING of
Newburyport, who was born at Salisbury in 1800, wrote
some short poems in his early years. Rev. S. P. HILL, a
native of Salem, and pastor of a church in Haverhill
about sixty years ago, also wrote some meritorious lines.
BENJAMIN FRANKLIN NEWHALL, who was born at Saugus
in 1802, and died there in 1863, wrote both prose and
poetry. Mrs. ANNE MILES, who was born at Salem in
1803, and died in 1879, is said to have written some
very fine lines. FITCH POOLE, who was born at Peabody
in 1803, and died there in 1873, wrote poetry for his
papers—the *Wizard* and the *Peabody Press*, of which
he was editor respectively. Oliver Wendell Holmes
once said that he regarded Mr. Poole as among the
brightest and most genial humorists in the country at
that time. He was the author of many satirical and
humorous ballads, and had a great local reputation forty
years ago. Rev. EDWIN MARTIN STONE, who was born
in 1805, and was a Congregational pastor in Beverly for
thirteen years, wrote poetry. Miss MARIA AUGUSTA FUL-
LER of Lynn, who was born there in 1806, and died in
1831, at the age of twenty-four, was talented and imag-

inative, and wrote some good lines over the signature of "Finella." She had a good education, and was possessed of fascinating manners, though her writings were plaintive and sad. Mrs. M. C. SPARKS, widow of Jared Sparks, and daughter of Hon. Nathaniel Silsbee of Salem, "printed, not published," a volume of verse, entitled " Hymns, Home, Harvard, " in 1883. WILSON FLAGG, the Essex county Thoreau, spent many of his early years in Beverly, and wrote several odes thereabout 1835. He afterward contributed to the *Boston Weekly Magazine*. He was son of Isaac Flagg, an old schoolmaster of Beverly, and died at Cambridge in 1884, at the age of seventy-eight. Mrs. HARRIET FOWLER, who is now very aged, and her daughter Miss HARRIET PUTNAM FOWLER, both of Danvers, have contributed poems to the papers. Miss Fowler has also published "Three Smoking Husbands," a little work on "Vegetarianism," and short stories. Rev. GEORGE B. CHEEVER, who was born at Hallowell, Me., in 1807, and graduated at Bowdoin College in 1825, was a minister in Salem, publishing, while there, the "American Common-Place Book of Poetry" in 1829, and "Studies in Poetry" in 1830. JOHN BARNARD, a native of Newburyport, where he now lives upward of eighty years of age, wrote over the signature of "The Rambler" quite a number of meritorious verses in his younger years, which were published in the *New Orleans Delta*, and other periodicals. The late venerable Rev. LOTHROP WITHINGTON, and also his grandson of the same name, wrote considerably and well for the Newburyport and other papers. The late

JOHN B. DERBY, a native of Salem, born about 1808, was poet of the class in Bowdoin College with which he graduated, read law in his native place, and wrote considerably in measure. He married, but his wife lived only a year, and his mind became clouded. Evidence of insanity runs all through his poems. He was for a while a patient in the McLean Asylum, with but little benefit. In 1834, he had a sickness, suffering greatly for a year, and losing temporarily the use of his legs. He afterward lived as a hermit in the wilds of New Hampshire, where he wrote a volume of poems, entitled "Musings of a Recluse," which was published in 1837. One of his poems, " A Dream, "ends as follows :—

> "Oh ! let me spread my wings for flight,
>   From pain and sorrow flee away;
> Escape the shadows of the night,
>   And soar to realms of endless day."

SOLOMON MOULTON, who was born at Lynn in 1808, and died of consumption in 1827, wrote some plaintive lines for *The Weekly Mirror* over the signature of "Lillie." Another of Lynn's writers is JOSEPH WARREN NYE, an aged gentleman, who has done more writing for occasions than any other poet in the county. He has published a volume of poems. Gen. HENRY K. OLIVER, who died at Salem in 1885, at the age of eighty-four, wrote considerable verse for the local press, and Gen. F. W. LANDER wrote for the *Atlantic Monthly*. JOHN OSBORNE SARGENT, brother of Epes Sargent, born at Gloucester in 1811, now residing winters in New York City and summers at Lenox, Mass., well known as "The

Berkshire Tanner," has written both prose and poetry.
Rev. JOHN PRINCE, who was born at Beverly in 1820,
and now resides in Washington, D. C., has written considerable poetry, and published, in 1845, at Essex, a
volume of verse, entitled "Rural Lays and Sketches, and
Other Poems,"and the journal called the *Essex Cabinet.*
He became a Universalist clergyman, and preached at Essex, South Hingham, and South Danvers, now Peabody,
in Massachusetts, and at Meredith Bridge, now Laconia,
in New Hampshire. He served several years in both
houses of the Massachusetts legislature. He removed
to Washington in 1862, and was for many years chief
of a division in the Treasury. He was also a lecturer,
and published discourses upon theological subjects and
temperance. He has been a contributor to the journals of Essex county, and of Boston and Washington,
having been for some years the regular Washington
correspondent of the *Boston Commonwealth.* In an
ode written for the consecration of a cemetery, he says
of the dead,

"With folded hands across the breast,
    With lips that move no more at will,
    And features calm,—they here shall rest,
    With upward look, serene and still."

Mr. Prince's daughter, Mrs. MARY PRINCE STORY of
Essex, has also written some poems for the *Boston Com-
monwealth.* Miss ELIZABETH H. WHITTIER, sister of our
Quaker poet, was the author of several short poems.
She died at Amesbury September 3, 1864. Mrs. SU-
SAN FRANCES CLAPP, wife of Rev. Dexter Clapp, pastor

of the East church in Salem, and daughter of Judge
Preston of Bangor, Me., wrote some good poetry for the
*Monthly Religious Magazine, Salem Gazette, Chris-
tian Examiner* and *Monthly Miscellany.* She died in
Salem, of a cancer, June 21, 1859, at the age of forty-
two, and her remains were laid to rest in Mount Auburn.
JOSHUA DANFORTH ROBINSON, who resided in Newburyport some years, being engaged in mercantile pursuits,
possessed genius as a writer, but produced very little. His
principal poem, entitled "The Little Boy that Died,"
found its way to every heart. It was first published in
the *Newburyport Daily Union*, anonymously, and was,
by many papers, into which it was copied, attributed to
the pen of Dr. Chalmers. Two of the stanzas are as
follows :—

> "I am all alone in my chamber now,
>   And the midnight hour is near,
> And the fagot's crack and the clock's dull tick
>   Are the only sounds I hear;
> And over my soul in its solitude
>   Sweet feelings of sadness glide;
> For my heart and my eyes are full when I think
>   Of the little boy that died.
>
> .   .   .   .   .
>
> "We shall all go home to our Father's house—
>   To our Father's house in the skies,
> Where the hope of our souls shall have no blight,
>   And our love no broken ties;
> We shall roam on the banks of the River of Peace,
>   And bathe in its blissful tide;
> And one of the joys of our heaven shall be
>   The little boy that died."

Mr. Robinson removed to Texas about 1860, to engage in agriculture, and, with several members of his
family, died of the cholera at San Antonio, in the summer of 1866. Mrs. ELIZABETH W. CHAPMAN of Rowley, now an aged lady, has written much for the local
papers, generally on religious subjects. Hon. ROBERT
RANTOUL, jr., of Beverly also wrote verse. Mrs. ELIZ-
ABETH CYNTHIA ELLSWORTH of Boston, a native of Essex county, who died at Boston in 1883, wrote hymns
of recognized merit. JAMES F. COLMAN published a
volume of verse at Boston in 1846, entitled "The Isl-
and Bride, and Other Poems." EDWIN JOCELYN, a
native of Danvers, and a school teacher in Salem, wrote
poetry for the *Salem Register* in 1851. Rev. VARNUM
LINCOLN of Andover has written several poems for the
Christian Leader. EBEN W. KIMBALL, Esq., of Salem,
a lawyer, wrote poetry for the *Salem Advertiser* forty
years ago over the name of "Topaz," as also did DANIEL
R. BECKFORD of Boston, formerly of Salem, over the
signature of " Amethyst." The late GILBERT CONANT,
a native and resident of Ipswich, wrote a number of
poems on natural subjects. Mrs. AUGUSTA HARVEY
WORTHEN of Lynn, formerly of Danvers, and originally
from New Hampshire has written a number of poems.
The following are extracts from her pretty lines entitled "The Cup Moss :"—

"These tiny red cups, this brilliant array
On this sober gray rock, what means this display?
Is a sideboard set for a humming bird?
Do these vases wait till his wine is poured?

.   .   .   .   .

"Here is one will hold just a single drop,
 And a rim like a rose wreath encircles the top;
 Does Queen Mab herself come here to sup?
 And is this her dainty drinking cup?
     .   .   .   .   .

"They never affect the coquettish toss
 Of their velvety cousin, the soft meadow moss;
 But they're prettier than even the moss that grows
 'Round the slender form of the pale moss rose.
     .   .   .   .   .

"No pleasure, think you, the gray rock knows,
 Nor pride in the midst of its stern repose,
 When, though south winds whisper of softer rest,
 Clings closer the moss to its granite breast?
 Does it not willingly, gladly impart
 The enduring strength of its brave old heart?
     .   .   .   .   .

". . . A blossoming wild rose, one morn,
 Hung over the moss with its sweet perfume
 Till the pale little creature caught its bloom.
     .   .   .   .   .

"A day and a night, and then it was gone;
 But the joy in the heart of the moss lives on,
 And nothing henceforth shall break the spell,
 For it caught the hue it loved so well."

Mrs. SARAH C. MAYO, while residing at Gloucester, wrote poetry. She was born in 1819, and died in 1848. JOSIAH F. KIMBALL of Lynn, who died in Boston February 3, 1889, at the age of sixty-seven, was a native of Ipswich, and a writer of poetry on miscellaneous subjects. His efforts were contributed to the *Semi-Weekly Reporter, Newburyport Herald, Commercial Bulletin, Lynn Transcript, Salem Gazette, Boston Common-*

wealth, Boston Traveller, Boston Herald, Bay State,
and other papers. He was a printer by trade, and was
publisher of the *Essex County Whig,* which was soon
afterward called *Lynn News.* Col. THOMAS WENTWORTH
HIGGINSON was born at Cambridge, Mass., in 1823,
graduated at Harvard College in 1841, and has written
poetry from time to time throughout his life. He was
ordained pastor of the First Congregational church in
Newburyport in 1847, and on account of his anti-slavery
preaching had to leave after a few years' service. He
afterward preached at Worcester, and left the ministry
in 1858. He was very prominent in the anti-slavery
conflict, and served in the army during the Rebellion.
He finally devoted himself to literature, publishing several volumes of essays, history, and biography. He has
just issued a volume of miscellaneous poems, entitled
"The Afternoon Landscape." Col. JOSEPH WARREN
FABENS, who was born at Salem in 1821, and was
United States consul at Cayenne, South America, for
several years, wrote a number of poems, which were
published in 1887 in a volume entitled "The Last Cigar,
and Other Poems," with portrait, and a biographical
preface by Julia Ward Howe. He wrote and published
in prose "The Camel Hunt," "Life on the Isthmus,"
and other books. In his youth he wrote verses for the
Salem papers, namely, the *Observer, Register,* and *Gazette.* Col. Fabens was an earnest supporter of the
project to annex the Island of Santo Domingo to the
United States. He died at Elizabeth, N. J., in 1875.
Mrs. ANTOINETTE PURINGTON of Lynn has published

a number of poems. AUSTIN PHELPS, who was professor of sacred rhetoric in the theological seminary at Andover from 1848 to 1866, is the author of a number of good hymns, and compiler of several hymn books. Miss REBECCA INGERSOLL DAVIS of East Haverhill has written considerable poetry. She is also a prose writer, and has published two volumes, entitled "Gleanings from Merrimac Valley," containing poems and historical and biographical sketches, which have become quite popular. G. L. STREETER of Salem wrote some creditable stanzas for the *Boston Transcript* in 1866 ; and H. B. SARGENT wrote poems for the *Atlantic Monthly* during the war of the Rebellion. Dr. WILLIAM H. BRIGGS, brother of Mrs. Caroline A. Mason, is another native writer of poetry. In his younger years he wrote for the *Salem Register*, and later for *Arthur's Home Gazette*. The late GEORGE INNIS, a printer of Newburyport, was also among our writers. Another was Mrs. MARY ANN CONANT, daughter of John Friend, and wife of Prof. George Conant. Her writings, both prose and verse, were much admired. She was born at Andover in 1829, was reared at Boxford, and taught school in Georgetown, Mass., and in Buffalo, N. Y. She assisted her husband in his school at Coshocton, Ohio, and at Alexander, N. Y., where she died, of heart disease, February 18, 1883, at the age of fifty-three. WASHINGTON VERY of Salem, brother of Rev. Jones Very, was a writer of verses. Reverends SAMUEL GILMAN, WILLIAM PARSONS LUNT, CHANDLER ROBBINS, and SAMUEL D. ROBBINS, wrote hymns. JAMES LAWRENCE WALES, who died in

Groveland some years since, wrote a number of poems for the *Georgetown Advocate*. Miss MARY ABIGAIL DODGE of Hamilton, the "Gail Hamilton" of literature, has also written some meritorious verses. She was daughter of James B. and Hannah (Stanwood) Dodge, and was born in Hamilton. S. EDWIN IRESON, Esq., who was for several years city solicitor of Lynn, where he was born in 1830, wrote several poems. He graduated at Harvard College in 1853, and died in Lynn about fifteen years ago. He had talent as a writer, which his frail constitution would not permit him to cultivate. He contributed to many periodicals, generally anonymously. Mrs. ANN E. PORTER of Newburyport has written poetry for many years. JOHN T. DEVEREUX of Salem published a collection of poems, which he had contributed to periodicals. EDWARD JOHNSON and DAVID N. JOHNSON, both of Lynn, have written poetry, the latter being the author of "Sketches of Lynn," and a translator of German poetry. Miss Anne G. Hale had two brothers, GEORGE HENRY HALE, born at Newburyport in 1831, dying there in 1850, and EDWARD HALE, born in 1835, dying in 1854, who wrote some graceful lines, the latter publishing his poems in the *Boston Museum, Knickerbocker Magazine, Christian Witness*, and other periodicals. JOSEPH A. BATCHELDER, Esq., of Middleton, wrote a number of poems many years ago. ALLEN PEABODY of Wenham was the " Bard of Enon" a score of years ago. GEORGE E. EMERY of Lynn is a prolific writer, not largely of poetry, but with merit. CHARLES STUART OSGOOD, Esq.,

born at Salem in 1839, register of deeds there, has written a few poems for the *Boston Transcript*. GEORGE
BANCROFT GRIFFITH of Woodfords, Me., born at Newburyport in 1841, and educated at Dummer Academy,
has been a contributor to the *Youth's Companion* and
St. Nicholas, and to the religious press. ISAAC BASSET
CHOATE, formerly of Lynn, and later of New York City,
and Akron, Ohio, wrote for the *Salem Gazette* in 1866,
and still contributes verses to the papers. N. ALLEN
LINDSEY of Marblehead has written poetry for the *Boston Transcript* and *Independent*. Miss MARCIA M.
SELMAN is another of the Marblehead writers. Mrs.
EMILY SHAW FORMAN and JOSEPH A. STEELE are two
more of Lynn's poets, and Mrs. MARY A. PARSONS of
Lynnfield Centre has written some poems. Miss EMILY
E. POOR of Ipswich, a native of Andover, has written
some good poetry for the *Portland Transcript, Christian Register, Congregationalist, Massachusetts Teacher*,
and other periodicals. In her war poem, entitled " An
Appeal to the North," occur the following lines :—

" Men of the North, arise ! shake off your palsied dreams,
Ye're sleeping o'er volcanic fires, whose fierce and lurid gleams
E'en now are flashing from the earth, which rocks beneath your
    tread,
And the rumbling of its pent-up wrath fills every heart with
    dread.

. . . .

Awake, fair Northern women, nor deem it not your sphere
To be brave and earnest for the right, nor the name 'strong-
    minded' fear;

No true woman can be other than pure, gentle and refined,
However brave her actions, however strong her mind !

  . . . .

O patriots, Christians, parents, men ! no longer sleep supine,
For your country, God, humanity need those strong, brave
  hearts of thine ! "

THOMAS H. RONAYNE, Esq., now a lawyer of New
York City, was formerly a resident of Lynn, and while
there wrote some poems for *The Pilot.*   Dr. FREDER-
ICK K. CROSBY, a dentist of Lynn, practising there in
1868 and 1869, wrote poetry for the *Lynn Transcript,*
Lynn Reporter, *Stewart's Quarterly,* and *Appleton's*
Journal. He was born at Newton, Mass., in 1845, and
died in 1874 at San Diego, Cal., whither he had gone
for his health. He graduated at the Philadelphia Den-
tal College in 1867, and on leaving Lynn practised for
a while at St. John, N. B.   A volume of his poems was
printed for private distribution, at Boston in 1876, with
the title "Into Light, and Other Poems."   HENRY
MIGHILL NELSON of Georgetown, AMANDA S. GEORGE
of Ipswich, and S. A. COBURN and Miss HARRIETTE O.
NELSON, both of Haverhill, wrote verse some years ago.
A volume of poetry, entitled "The Ruler's Daughter,
and Other Poems," by CAROLINE R. DERBY of Salem
was "printed, not published," at Salem in 1877. She was
the daughter of E. Hersey Derby.   She also published
a novel, entitled "Salem ; or a Tale of the Seventeenth
Century," and a series of tales in *Harper's Maga-*
zine, under the *nom de plume* of " D. R. Castleton."
Mrs. RUTH M. WEBSTER of West Boxford is another

writer of poetry. E. F. MERRILL of Lynn wrote for the *Boston Transcript* in 1877. CHARLES E. HOAG, Esq., of Peabody, a lawyer, and the editor of the *Peabody Reporter* and the *American Citizen*, is also a writer of poetry. CLARA F. BERRY of North Andover published considerable poetry in 1870; and in 1877 JAMES DAVIS, Esq., judge of the police court of Gloucester, issued a little volume, entitled "Pleasant Water," a song of the sea and shore. ARTHUR SHERBURNE HARDY, born in Andover August 13, 1847, professor of mathematics in Dartmouth College, has published a poem entitled "Francesca de Rimini." He was in school at Neuchatel, Switzerland, during the twelfth and thirteenth years of his life, and in 1863 travelled through Spain. On his return home he graduated from Phillips' Academy, was one year at Amherst College, and graduated at the United States Military Academy in 1869. He became instructor at West Point, and afterward entered upon his duties at Hanover. He is also a novelist. Mrs. E. G. LAKE of Salem wrote poetry for the papers many years ago. Miss CHARLOTTE E. RICKER of Topsfield, afterward of Peabody, has written several good poems. Rev. JOSIAH GREENE WILLIS, who was born in 1853, becoming a journalist, and afterward pastor of the Congregational church at Lanesville, in Gloucester, now being settled at Dana, Mass., has contributed verses to the *Springfield Republican* and other prominent periodicals. The following is a selection from his popular poem entitled "Golden Rule Religion :"—

14

"The creeds are big with theologic lore
From men whose knowledge was a wondrous store
Of things concerning God's most holy writ
Which doth transcend all human skill or wit.
But life is real, in both act and speech—
'Tis hard to practise, though with ease we preach;
We have the sum of all creeds understood
If we love God, and live for doing good.

.   .   .   .

"Do we the worthy poor both clothe and feed,
Ministering to their discouragement and need?
We know it is a blest and great employ,
To speak and act toward giving others joy:
What hallowed years the gentle Saviour spent
As he among the poor and lonely went!
That piety whose power none can refute
Makes glad the suffering and the destitute.

"The Golden Rule, not for God's Day alone
When earthly saints assemble at his throne;
Not merely for the church, within whose walls
The preacher's voice in prayer or sermon calls.
But this rule ought to guide us, day and night;
It is divine—we know that it is right,
Whatever be our church, or names, or creeds,
May it control our language and our deeds!"

Mrs. KATIE D. KILPATRICK, formerly Miss May of Lynn,
now residing in Beaverhead Valley, Montana, has written
several poems for the local newspapers.   From that
entitled "Summer Morning" are extracted the following
stanzas :—

"The sunlight falls on the bee,
  And he sips
  As he tips
The nectarian flasks,
  Till it tasks
E'en himself to return o'er the lea.

   .   .   .   .   .

"The sunlight falls at my door,
  And I look
  From the book
Of earth's wonderful grace
  To His face
In whose presence is light evermore."

CLARENCE W. CLAPP of Danvers, formerly of Topsfield, has written much verse. GEORGE F. HARTSON of Salem and AGNES FIELDING of Beverly contributed poetry to the *Salem Gazette* in 1878. Miss ANNIE B. BENSEL, also of Lynn, sister of James Berry Bensel, has written a few poems. Miss EMILY GREENE WETHERBEE, a school teacher in Lawrence, has written poems for the *Boston Journal, Boston Globe, Boston Transcript,* and *Journal of Education.* GEORGE W. JONES of Salem has published poetry. His "Jupiter Tonans" is as follows :—

" O, the naughty baby,—we had had to put her
  In the corner till she'd promise to be good.
    With her flaxen hair awry,
    Angry tear-drops in each eye,
  There the wilful little rebel stood."

" Silence for a moment; then she slowly turned around,
  Looked at us, and tossed her little head—
    'This time you have had your way;
    Just wait till another day,
  Then we'll see,' was all the baby said."

FRANK ROLAND WHITTEN of Lynn, who was born there in 1863, has done considerable literary work, having published poems in the *Portland Transcript* and local papers. The following is his poem entitled "Flood-Tide :—

"I hear the rising waters where they urge
　The raging, noisy and tumultuous surge
　　To climb the sandy reaches of the shore.
　The tide is up, and miles of marshes low
　Are buried 'neath resistless overflow,
　　While ocean chants with hoarse, victorious roar.

" Each pool and rivulet grows broad and free,
　Swells and throbs high responsive to the sea.
　　No sound is heard save that melodious surf,
　In undertone sonorous and sublime,—
　That changeless voice, as old as earth or time—
　　Where leagues of ocean smite the trembling turf.

"And like those restless waves methinks is life,
　Filling the world with fierce and noisy strife.
　　Unconquered, yet unconquering are we,
　Beating in vain the walls of our desire—
　Now hushed in peace, now frantic in our ire—
　　Man's life is strange and awful, like the sea."

Miss ANNIE F. BURNHAM, formerly of Georgetown, is the author of some fine lines. She has written many juvenile articles for the *Youth's Companion, Wide Awake,* and other periodicals ; one of her little poems, entitled "Resting," which she composed several years ago, being as follows :—

" ' I want to be holded and rested.'
  O little one! do you see
  How my thought leaps into expression,
    As I echo your innocent plea?—
  How I come unto my Father,
    As you come unto me?

" 'I want to be holded and rested;'
    I am tired in heart and brain;
  Sick with a nameless sadness,
    Weary with life's old pain
  That, hushed into silence, awakens
    And cries in my soul again.

" I bless the dear child for her lesson,
    I follow the footsteps she trod;
  Not songs, but the infinite Silence,
    His love in my heart shed abroad.
  I have crept, in my weariness, closer
    To the restful heart of my God."

Miss Lida Lewis Watson, now of Boston, formerly of Haverhill, where most of her life has been spent, has written a large number of poems for the *Boston Globe.* Miss Henrietta E. Dow and Miss Bessie Bland are two of Lynn's younger writers of poetry. George F. Barry, youngest son of Darius Barry, and brother of Eugene Barry, born at Lynn in 1859, had fine literary tastes, and contributed poetry to the *Lynn Transcript.* He died at Lynn in 1883, of malarial fever. Miss Ida G. Rust of Topsfield has written several poems which are meritorious. J. Henry Dwyer is another of Lynn's young writers. Miss Nellie L. Saunders, a young lady of Lanesville, Gloucester, has written a number of poems for the Gloucester and Salem papers.   Miss HELEN S. BARNJUM, a young lady of Lynnfield, has written some pretty things.   Miss ETHEL M. RYDER of Salem has displayed considerable talent in writing poetry.   Her literary name is "Maude."   Misses CORA E. GROVER of Salem and IRENE CHAPLIN TYLER of Georgetown have also written and published some creditable poems.